"I'm sorry about what happened last night.

"I had no idea my dancing with someone would cause such a problem."

"Yeah, well, this is Montana. Not New York," he said.

His response stabbed at her. "Are you saying dancing causes issues in Montana?"

"A beautiful woman causes issues anywhere," Gage said.

"I'm not that beautiful," she retorted.

Gage looked at her in disbelief. "That's a matter of opinion. Just do me a favor and stay away from the bar the next few days. I don't have the manpower to handle the riots you cause."

"Are you saying this is my fault?"

"I'm saying you underestimated your power," he said.

Lissa felt her frustration build inside her. Her whole body roared with heat. "You're being a jerk. A complete jerk," she told him. She poked her finger against his hard chest repeatedly. "If you think I'm so beautiful, why don't you stop being such an idiot and kiss me?"

Dear Reader,

I've always had a fascination with Western sheriffs, and I was thrilled to have the opportunity to write the love story for Sheriff Gage Christensen. He has been totally focused on helping the citizens of Rust Creek Falls get back on their feet after disaster struck. He has been carrying around a lot of unnecessary guilt, too. What he needs is a woman who will get under his skin, bother him a little, remind him he's a man— a *good* man.

Volunteer Lissa Roarke from Manhattan hits him, and the town, like a thunderbolt. She's come to Rust Creek Falls to make a difference and nothing will stop her from accomplishing her goal. Lissa has always been fascinated with cowboys and she decides this is a great time to learn that the myth about them really is just a myth. But what if the reality is more than she could have dreamed?

I hope you'll enjoy their story. I would love to hear your thoughts. Please email me at leannebbb@aol.com.

Happy reading!

Leanne Banks

www.LeanneBanks.com

The Maverick &
the Manhattanite

—

Leanne Banks

HARLEQUIN® SPECIAL EDITION®

Special thanks and acknowledgment to Leanne Banks for her contribution to the Montana Mavericks: Rust Creek Cowboys continuity.

Recycling programs
for this product may
not exist in your area.

ISBN-13: 978-0-373-65763-6

THE MAVERICK & THE MANHATTANITE

Printed in U.S.A.

www.Harlequin.com

Books by Leanne Banks

Harlequin Special Edition

Silhouette Special Edition

Silhouette Desire

Other titles by Leanne Banks
available in ebook format.

LEANNE BANKS

is a *New York Times* and *USA TODAY* bestselling author who is surprised every time she realizes how many books she has written. Leanne loves chocolate, the beach and new adventures. To name a few, Leanne has ridden an elephant, stood on an ostrich egg (no, it didn't break), gone parasailing and indoor skydiving. Leanne loves writing romance, because she believes in the power and magic of love. She lives in Virginia with her family and a four-and-a-half-pound Pomeranian named Bijou. Visit her website, www.leannebanks.com.

This book is dedicated to Susan Litman.
Thanks for letting me join the Maverick train again!

Chapter One

My suitcase is packed and I'm ready for my assignment as a lead coordinator for Bootstraps, a charitable organization based in New York City. I'm getting ready to travel from my world to a totally different one. I'm trading subways, theater, high fashion and rush hour crowds for a small town in Montana that's been nearly destroyed by a flood. No more cushy apartment or paved sidewalks for me. I'll be facing mud—a lot of it. I expect I won't find a lot of Wall Street types in a town called Rust Creek. But there will be cowboys—and I've always been curious about cowboys....

— *Lissa Roarke*

Lissa's roommate, Chelsea, swirled her glass of red wine as she picked up one of the boots from Lissa's suitcase. Chelsea eyed it with disgust. "I can't believe you're actually going to wear something with the label *John Deere*."

"Hey, these are great," Lissa said. "They're weather resistant and the lining is moisture wicking and breathable. They've got removable orthotics, a tempered-steel shank and a rubber outsole."

"But they're ugly," Chelsea said and dropped the boot back into Lissa's open suitcase. She took a deep sip of wine. "I know you're into your job and you want to help people, but are you sure this is a good idea? There must be plenty you can still do here."

"This is a huge opportunity for me. I'll be the lead coordinator. Besides, my rent will be covered and you'll get to rule our little roost," Lissa said, giving her roommate a hug.

"But I'll miss you," Chelsea admitted. "And I've worked so hard to improve your style quotient."

Chelsea worked for a women's fashion magazine and believed one of her missions in life was to help everyone dress with more style and flair. She glanced in Lissa's suitcase again and gave a disapproving sniff. "Couldn't you at least include a Givenchy or Hermès scarf? A Burberry sweater?

Remember what I've told you. Just a few stand-out pieces can really make a difference."

Lissa smothered a chuckle. "Chelsea, I need to be ready to work. I need to give these people a strong impression that I'm there to help them if they're going to take me seriously. They haven't received enough national attention or help. No rock stars are holding concerts for them, and most of their town was practically wiped out, from what I've heard."

Chelsea sighed. "True, I suppose," she said and took another sip of wine. "You're such a good soul. I really will miss you."

"You won't have to share the bathroom," Lissa reminded her.

"Well, when you put it that way," Chelsea said. "Ciao. I'm putting a little prezzie in your suitcase for a time you may need it. Probably tomorrow night," she muttered under her breath. "No peeking."

"You don't need to give me any presents," Lissa said.

"Oh, I do. I have very little conscience, but I can't ignore true north on this one."

While Chelsea moved through the small apartment wearing a morose expression, Lissa doublechecked her list and made last-minute preparations for her trip. She was halfnervous and totally excited. Her first assignment as lead coordinator.

She'd never be able to explain it to Chelsea, or her family of high achievers, for that matter, but Lissa had grown weary of life in the city and she was looking forward to being in a totally different environment. Her daily journal entries had grown stale and depressing. Her parents had always cautioned her not to put too much energy into her passion for writing. They thought she should focus on something more practical. Working for Bootstraps had offered her the unique opportunity to help people and also blog about her experiences on their website.

Although she knew her temporary stay in Montana would be challenging, she was looking forward to fresh air, big blue skies and wide-open spaces.

And cowboys. She wouldn't admit it to anyone else, but she'd had a fascination with cowboys for a long time. She wanted to know more about the real kind of cowboy, and apparently Montana was full of them. Lissa felt a twinge of guilt when she thought that Chelsea believed Lissa was being so self-sacrificing by going to Montana.

Lissa closed her eyes and brushed the unwelcome feeling aside. Her first duty was to help the community of Rust Creek Falls, and she was determined to make a difference. Cowboys were just the cherry on top of the assignment.

* * *

In his office, Sheriff Gage Christensen took another sip of coffee as he prowled the small area and listened to Charlene Shelton, a volunteer senior deputy, give her weekly report on how the elderly in his jurisdiction were faring. As soon as he'd begun serving as sheriff, Gage had learned it was a lot easier to appoint a volunteer to check on folks than wait for calls. "I've made all my calls. Everyone is mostly fine. Teresa Gilbert may need a ride to the doctor next week, so we'll need a volunteer driver for that. The only one who didn't answer or call me back was Harry Jones, but you know he's a stubborn one. Always has been. Ever since his wife died last year, he's just gotten worse."

"I'll get Will to check on Harry," he said, speaking of his deputy. "He won't mind."

"I'm still worried about all the people still stuck in trailers since the flood," she clucked. "Winter is coming and I can't believe those cheap trailers will withstand our blizzards."

Gage felt his neck tighten with tension. He didn't disagree with Charlene, but it would take time to put the rural town back together after the flash flood they'd experienced. "We're all working on it, Charlene. In fact, we've got a charity-relief woman coming in from the East. She should arrive this afternoon."

"From the East?" Charlene echoed, clearly enjoying receiving this bit of news. Gage figured she would be burning up the phone wires as soon as they finished the call. "How is someone from the East going to know what to do here? Where's she from?"

Gage hesitated. "New York."

Silence followed. "Well, I suppose they have experience with flooding, but we don't have subways or high-rises."

"I know, but we're not in a position to turn down help. I've been tapping every connection I can find. Some people are responding. Others are already booked. We need to get as much done as possible since winter will hit early."

"Yes, we're in hard times. If only Hunter McGee was still with us," she said.

The mention of the former mayor's name stabbed him. There was never a day that passed that he didn't think about the mayor's death during the storm. Gage blamed himself. His parents had talked him into taking a quick trip to a rodeo out of town and Hunter had agreed to cover for Gage. The flood hit and Hunter had rushed out in response to a call. A tree had fallen on his car and he'd died of a heart attack.

"No one can replace Hunter," Gage said.

"That's true, but we're lucky we have you as sheriff, Gage. You've been working nonstop to help us," Charlene said.

"There's always more to do," he said.

"Well, I'll bring you a pie the next time I come into town. A single man needs a pie every now and then," she said.

Gage looked at the baked goods piled on a table next to the dispatcher's desk. "You don't have to do that, Charlene. We all appreciate the work you do with the calls you make each week."

"Oh, it's nothing," she said. "I can bake a pie in my sleep."

Gage swallowed a sigh. "Thanks for making those calls. Take care, now."

At that moment, he heard the sound of a husky, feminine laugh and wondered who it was. It was a sexy sound that distracted him.

Gage glanced outside his office and saw his twenty-one-year-old deputy, Will Baker, walk into the office with a slim redhead by his side. The woman was a head-snapper with her fiery hair, long legs and confident air.

"Hey, uh, Gage, this is Lissa Roarke, the relief worker you told me to pick up from the airport. She needs someone to show her around town. I can do it."

Gage tore his gaze from the woman's eyes and bit back a smile. He wasn't at all surprised that Will was volunteering to show the pretty New Yorker around. He was practically drooling all over the woman. "That's okay. Vickie," he said, referring to this dispatcher, "needs to leave early, so I'd like you to fill in at the dispatcher desk for a couple hours."

Disappointment shadowed Will's face. "Oh, well, if you need me for anything, Lissa, give me a call. I wrote down my cell number for you. Call me anytime."

"Thank you, Will, and thank you for picking me up from the airport and taking me to the rooming house before bringing me here. You're a much better driver than most of the ones I deal with in the city."

Will stood a little taller. "We take our driving seriously out here."

Gage cleared his throat. "Will, thank you for picking up Miss Roarke. Vickie's waiting, okay." He moved toward the New Yorker and extended his hand. "I'm the sheriff, Gage Christensen. We appreciate your help."

"Please, call me Lissa," she said in a voice that held a hint of a sexy rasp. She returned his handshake. Her hand was small and soft. He had a hard time imagining her smooth, uncalloused hand doing hard labor. Her long red hair fell in a mass of curls to her shoulders and he liked the fact that she didn't seem to care about taming it. Maybe she wasn't as high maintenance as he feared. He'd met a few city women and most of them had seemed obsessed with their hair and nails. Her blue eyes glinted with curiosity and intelligence.

"Call me Gage," he said. "Do you need something to eat before I show you around?" He cocked his head toward the table near the dispatcher's desk. "People are always dropping off food for us. It's generous, but if I ate everything they bring in, I'd be as big as a barn. Sometimes I wonder if they're secretly trying to kill me," he joked in a low voice.

Lissa gave a light laugh. "I'm sure they're just showing their appreciation. I'm not hungry, though, because I ate during my layover. I'm anxious to see Rust Creek Falls. I visited Thunder Canyon when one of my cousins got married and it was beautiful."

"I better warn you that Rust Creek is a lot different from Thunder Canyon. Thunder Canyon has a first-class resort and a lot of shops. We have the minimum requirements here. For everything else, we have to head out of town. Things aren't nearly as picturesque since the flood here, either."

"That's okay," she said. "I have some experience with floods myself after living in New York City."

"I can't deny you that. You've had some natural disasters that looked like real messes on the news," he said and led her outside to his patrol car.

"Trust me. They were worse in person," she said and slid into the passenger seat.

Even though he wasn't all that confident that a lady from Manhattan was going to be able to help Rust Creek much, Gage was determined to be gracious. He had a hard time believing this city girl would really understand the needs of a small town. He drove down the street, pointing out the businesses that had mostly survived the flood. "We got lucky that some of our important buildings didn't get hit by the flood. The Masonic Hall," he said, gesturing to the structure as he turned onto North Main Street. "And thank goodness Crawford's General Store dodged that bullet. We get everything from feed to groceries there. And the church is still intact. By the way, the reverend is a good man and he'll be a good resource for you."

"That's good to know," Lissa said. "I'll try to meet him as soon as I can."

Taking a turn, he headed in a different direction. "One of the biggest losses was the elementary school. Teachers are holding classes in their homes. The town just doesn't have the money to rebuild."

"That's terrible," she said, making notes in a small notebook. "I'd like to make that a priority in terms of raising funds."

"This is the flood zone. Most of the houses were lost or damaged on these streets, including my sister's house."

"Can we stop so I can take a look inside the homes?"

"Sure," he said, pulling his car to the side of the road. He took her inside an unlocked house.

"Wow, the door isn't locked. Have you had trouble with looting?" she asked.

"Not so much. People took their valuables when they moved in with family or into the area where most of the trailers are," he said.

She nodded as she stepped inside and looked around. She tapped on the wooden floor with her foot. "This is good," she said as she looked around the bare room. "They've pulled out most of the sources for mold. Furniture, draperies. Even pulled out the dry wall and insulation."

"Some people cooperated and others just took off. We moved out the furniture next door, but the owners haven't touched the drywall."

She bit her lip. "That makes things more challenging, but I have some mold specialists coming in during the next few days. They'll make assessments and start work on our top priority places."

"I was wondering how you were going to get any professionals here since we're in the middle of nowhere. We've taxed our contacts in Thunder Canyon and Kalispell to the max, but those folks need to make a living, too. They can't work for free forever," he said.

She looked at him and nodded. "That's why

I'm here—to fill in those gaps. I remember reading about the trailer village. I've been able to get a few more for the specialists to share since they'll be around for a while. I'm going to have weekly volunteer groups staying at the church. Can you show me more of the damaged areas?"

"Sure," he said as she walked past him to leave the house. Despite her work boots, he noticed she had a nice little wiggle in her walk and she smelled more like a woman than a girl. Her dark and spicy scent was at odds with her fresh face and natural hair. She was more practical than he'd expected, Gage thought. She could be distracting and he didn't need that.

Gage drove out toward several ranches that had been damaged and had lost animals and he noticed Lissa continued to take notes. "Such a shame, but we're here to make it better. It's amazing how this seemed to happen in an instant. When New York flooded, at least we got some notice. Did you have any damage at your ranch?"

"My first floor was pretty much ruined. I lost a lot of personal papers and some photographs. I'm living in a temporary trailer at the moment," he said.

"Oh, I'm so sorry," she said, sympathy sliding through her voice like cool water on hot skin. "That must have been horrible."

Gage thought of the mayor who'd died in the

flood and everything inside him refused her kindness. "I got off easy," he snapped. "Some people lost their lives."

"Yes, of course," she said in an apologetic tone. "I didn't mean to—"

"I think you've probably seen enough to get you started. I'll take you back to the rooming house," he said tersely. As much as Gage wanted help for Rust Creek, he hadn't expected that being around the relief worker would remind him of all he'd been unable to do to help the people stranded by the flood because he'd been out of town. He'd spent every spare minute since the flood trying to help citizens get back on their feet, but the process was slow. Too slow for him.

Lissa climbed the creaky wooden steps to her room, feeling as if someone had taken the wind out of her sails. She'd started out the day filled with hope and determination, and even though the lingering devastation from the flood tugged at her, she'd felt optimistic as the sheriff showed her around.

Of course, it didn't hurt that he was tall and lean with muscles in all the right places, and he walked with a sexy, confident stroll that she suspected could turn into a fast run at the right moment. She liked his deep voice. Everything about him seemed *sure*. He might have his doubts and regrets about a few things, but Lissa sensed that Gage was okay in his own skin and didn't waste time wondering what people thought of him.

At the same time, his brooding gaze suggested a bit of sadness. She could tell he felt the burden of helping his community since the flood. She just wished she hadn't set him off with her sympathy for his own property loss. She should have known better. Rust Creek Falls had been suffering for months and Gage had a firsthand view of most of it.

Opening the door to the bedroom that would be her home for the next month, she glanced at the comfy-looking bed, chest of drawers, minifridge and coffeemaker. She was surprised to see a sandwich, chips and water on a tray for her with a note. "Thought you could use this after your long day. Let us know how we can help. Melba."

Lissa smiled. The thoughtfulness of Melba Strickland, the boardinghouse's owner, soothed her. This never would have happened to her in Manhattan. That was for sure. She tugged off her boots and went to the tiny bathroom to wash her hands and splash her face. All she wanted was to jump into her pj's, gobble down that sandwich and hit the sack. She opened her suitcase on the luggage rack and decided she'd unpack some other time. Digging down into the bottom, she found a box she couldn't remember packing. She pulled it out and opened it: two bottles of red wine. Lissa laughed. This must have been her roommate's gift.

Shaking her head, she put the box in her suitcase and pulled out her pj's. She didn't need wine. She needed a good night of sleep and the shot of optimism she hoped it would bring.

Gage didn't pull into his dirt driveway until after eleven o'clock. He stopped by the Martins' ranch, where he was helping Bob Martin redo the kitchen floor. The family hoped to be back in the house by Thanksgiving, but it was going to be close. Gage wasn't a certified plumber or electrician, but growing up with his dad had provided him with a lot of practical do-it-yourself knowledge.

He would ask Lissa Roarke if she could send her mold specialists over to the Martins. He thought of her and her long, curly hair and upbeat attitude. Inhaling deeply, he could almost smell her perfume.

Gage scowled at himself. What was he thinking? He'd just met Lissa and he could tell she was city through and through. Not at all his type. He'd dated a couple city girls during his early twenties who'd visited relatives in Rust Creek Falls, and he'd quickly learned that the women didn't have any staying power and needed more amusements than this small town could offer.

Stepping out of his car, he felt a chilly wind sweep through him. He shivered and hustled to the trailer he was living in now. If Gage had devoted himself to repairing his own home, he could have been in it a month ago, but it just didn't seem right to him. Entire families had been uprooted by the flood, so he spent most evenings trying to give those most affected a hand. Even though people were in need, they were more than willing to help their neighbors. That was a fact of life in Rust Creek and it was one of the reasons he'd allowed himself to be talked into running for sheriff.

There may have been times when he'd thought about leaving Montana, but his roots here ran deep. His family and the people were important to him. Ranching was in his blood. Gage stepped inside the trailer and felt the wind shake and rattle through his metal home. Chuckling to himself, he rubbed his hands together before he turned on his coffeemaker. Sometimes he felt like he was living in a tin can. He would get around to fixing his own home after he'd helped more of the families who were suffering.

Gage pulled off his hat and grabbed a pair of pajamas out of one of the few drawers in the trailer. Still cold, he stood over the coffeemaker until the brown liquid made its way to the carafe. Even with the long hours he was pulling he still sometimes had a hard time falling asleep, so he'd started drinking decaf at night. He sure as hell didn't need one more reason to keep him awake.

He poured a cup of the hot coffee then sank onto the sofa that sat across from his television. Turning on the TV, he prepared to lose himself in a ballgame. For a few minutes before he fell asleep, he would think about something besides the way so many of his people were suffering. He watched for several moments before his eyes started to drift closed. He blinked, realizing he was more tired than he'd thought.

Gage brushed his teeth and washed his face, then pulled out the sleep sofa and sank onto the bed. It wasn't the best bed, but it felt good at the moment. He listened to the game with his eyes closed for a few moments then turned off the TV. Sighing, he forced himself not to think about what he had on his plate tomorrow. Instead, a vision of a red-haired woman sneaked into his mind like smoke under a door.

Gage shook his head, willing the image away.

Lissa dragged herself out of bed, started the coffeemaker in the room and stumbled into the shower. It would take a few days for her to get used to the time zone change. It might only be two hours different from New York, and she might be an early riser, but five-thirty a.m. was a little too early for her. Inhaling a cup of coffee, she pulled on a set of long underwear, jeans and a sweater, as she ran through a mental list of what she wanted to accomplish today. Hoping she would succeed after riling the good sheriff, she brushed her teeth and put on a little lip gloss, then headed out of her room.

She smelled the scent of fresh coffee brewing along with something cinnamony baking in the oven and bacon frying. Lissa drooled. She'd planned to grab some yogurt from the local store.

A woman's voice called out to her. "Breakfast is almost ready. Come on in to the kitchen."

Lissa stepped into the warm room, catching sight of Melba Strickland, the eighty-something-year-old owner of the rooming house, removing crispy bacon from a cast iron skillet. "How do you like your eggs, honey?"

"Oh, you don't need to do that," Lissa said, noticing a couple of men at the breakfast table. "I planned to grab a bite on my way to the sheriff's office."

"No need for that when you can eat the best breakfast in town," Melba said, then shot Lissa an assessing glance from behind her glasses. "Besides, you look like you could use a little fattening up, and breakfast is included with your room. Sunny-side up or scrambled?"

"Scrambled, thank you," Lissa said, smiling at the take-charge woman.

"Go ahead and get yourself some coffee," Melba said, nodding toward the coffeemaker with mugs beside it. "There's orange juice, too, if you like. What do you have up your sleeve today?"

"Getting more information about the damage from the flood and trying to get a better feel for the layout of the county. I have a mold specialist coming in tomorrow. I'm hoping that since Montana is usually dry that it won't be the kind of problem we had with Hurricane Sandy."

Melba shook her head. "Trouble is, not everyone was willing to give up their furniture. If I said it once, I said it a hundred times—you have to get all the wet stuff *out* of the house, or you're just asking for more trouble. But I'm an old woman. I don't know anything." Melba plopped the scrambled eggs onto a plate along with a large portion of bacon and a huge cinnamon roll. "There you go. Eat up."

"Oh, that's entirely too—" Lissa stopped at the hard glance Melba threw at her. "Looks delicious. Thank you," she said, wondering if there was a hungry dog close by with whom she could share all the food.

She sat down next to an older man who had cleaned his plate. "Hello. I'm Lissa Roarke."

The man nodded. "Nice to meet you. I'm Gene Strickland, Melba's husband."

"I don't suppose you're still hungry," she said in a low voice.

He shook his head and chuckled. "No chance. But I'll distract her when you're done. You might wanna fix your own plate from now on. Melba thinks women are too skinny these days and she's on a mission to change that."

"Thanks for the tip," Lissa said. She hadn't wanted to offend the rooming house owner the second day she'd arrived in the state.

While Gene drank his coffee, Lissa finished her eggs, a slice of bacon and a few bites of the delicious cinnamon roll. When she could eat no more, she nodded in Gene's direction.

He nodded in return. "Hey Melba, I think we might have a leak in the roof. You want me to fix it?"

Melba frowned. "We don't have a leak in the roof. We better not have a leak in the roof," she said, putting her hands on her hips. "Even if we did, I wouldn't let you go climbing on top of the house at your age. Have you gone crazy? You show me what you're talking about, Gene."

Gene smiled and rose from the table. "I think it's on the northeast side," he said. "Let's take a look."

"Bless you, bless you," Lissa whispered and quickly rose and wrapped the rest of her cinnamon roll to eat later.

Walking out of the rooming house, she felt a hint of moisture in the cold air. She glanced up at the sky. She hadn't checked the weather, but she supposed that with those clouds, anything was possible. Shrugging, she headed down the street to the sheriff's office. The weather wasn't going to stop her today.

As she stepped into the building that housed the sheriff's office, she saw Gage putting on his Stetson and looking as if he were preparing to leave.

"Good morning," she said.

"Mornin'," he said in return. "I just got a call about an accident, so I won't be able to show you around today."

Will immediately piped up. "I can do it," he offered.

"You have to give the home-safety class for the school kids. Remember? You'll be busy all day going to all those different places they're holding class since we lost the school."

Will made a face. "I forgot."

"Good thing I didn't. Those teachers would have been ticked off at both of us if you hadn't shown up," Gage said.

"Well, what are you going to do with Lissa?" Will asked. "You can't just leave her stranded."

Gage sighed. "Maybe I can get Gretchen Paul to cart her around today."

Mildly offended by the word *cart,* Lissa shook

her head. "Oh, I don't want to be any trouble. Perhaps I could rent a car."

Gage and Will glanced at each other. "Not unless you want to go back to the airport and get it," Gage said.

"I don't know. Melba at the rooming house might let Lissa use her car. She might not even charge her," Will said.

"Not a good idea since she doesn't know her way around the country. Will, you need to remember Lissa isn't used to being in a rural place. No telling what might happen if she doesn't have someone to help her," Gage said.

Lissa's stomach knotted at his inference that she couldn't handle the job she was sent to do. "I think you're exaggerating. It's not as if this is Antarctica or outer Mongolia. Most of the roads I'll be driving on will be paved, and Rust Creek Falls isn't known for its violence."

"That may be true, but it's still a lot different than Manhattan and you just got here. You just sit tight. We'll figure out something by this afternoon. I need to head out," Gage said and left her staring after him.

Sit tight? I don't think so, Lissa thought. "Thanks for the tip, Will."

"Hey, maybe you better not do that," Will said. "Gage made a good point. You don't know your way around," he said, a worried look crossing his young face.

"I can read a map," she said, although she would have been much more comfortable with a reliable GPS. "I'll be fine."

Chapter Two

Lissa had been just fine until snow had started to fall and the roads turned slippery. After visiting a mom of three on the list Bootstraps had provided for her who needed new carpet and furniture, Lissa wobbled down the winding side road in Melba's eighteen-year-old Buick. Beggars couldn't be choosers, but Lissa wondered how Melba could possibly use such a vehicle with Montana's treacherous winters.

The snow pelted against the windshield and Lissa gripped the steering wheel so tightly her knuckles were white. The car veered to the center of the road and she immediately pulled it back into her lane. If she could just get to the main road, she thought she would be okay.

Suddenly, a deer appeared in front of her. Her heart jumped and she instinctively slammed on the brakes. The car went into a spin that seemed to go on forever. She struggled to gain control then felt the sickening sensation of the massive Buick tilting toward a ditch.

"No, no, no," she pleaded, willing the car back on the road.

Gravity won and the car slid headfirst into the ditch, stopping with an ugly jerk that yanked her head forward before the seat belt wrenched her back against the seat. It took a few seconds for Lissa to remember to breathe. As she gasped for air, willing her heart to stop pounding, she took inventory of herself, wiggling her shoulders and legs. Everything seemed okay, although the seat belt was holding her so tightly it felt like a vise. Pushing aside the discomfort, she glanced around and tried to figure out how to get out of the ditch. She opened the door to get out, but there wasn't enough room between the side of the ditch for her to open it all the way. Lissa glanced at the other side and grimly noticed that she had succeeded in wedging herself perfectly in the ditch, a feat she wouldn't have been able to accomplish if she'd intentionally tried.

She groaned. Lissa *really* didn't want to call the

sheriff. She could see the scowls and disapproval coming and she couldn't blame him. If she'd followed his advice, she wouldn't be in this mess. Frowning, she realized Gage wasn't the only lawman she could call. Will had given her his number. She could call the deputy and deal with Gage's displeasure another time. She was sick enough at the thought that she'd damaged Melba's car.

Lissa pulled Will's card from her purse and punched in his number. The call went directly to voice mail and she remembered Gage had said something about Will speaking about safety to the elementary children. Lissa reluctantly left a message and decided to wait for him to return the call.

She cut the engine and pulled out her tablet to make notes, but she glanced at the time every other minute. It was just after three o'clock. If Will didn't call soon, she was going to have to call Gage. She couldn't stay out here all night. Who knew how much more snow would fall in this surprise storm? She was already starting to feel trapped.

Her cell finally rang after eighteen minutes. She immediately answered. "Will?"

"Yes, Miss—Lissa," he said. "You said you've had a problem. What can I do for you?"

"Well, I'm in Melba Strickland's car on Route 563," she said and swallowed her pride. "And I'm stuck in a ditch."

Will gave a low whistle. "Are you injured?"

"No," she said. "But I'm going to need some serious help getting out of this ditch."

"Okay, sit tight. We'll take care of you. It may take a few minutes to get there since I'm on the other side of the county."

"Thank you," she said, relief spilling through her. "I really appreciate it."

"It's what I do," Will said. "See you soon."

Lissa slumped back against the seat and took a deep breath. As soon as she got out of this mess, she was going to rent an SUV with the best GPS available. She just hated that she'd let Melba down by wrecking her car.

Twenty-five minutes later, a male voice called to her outside her window. "Will. Thank goodness," she whispered and started the car. She pushed the button to lower the window. "Will?" she called, pleased that the snow had slowed to a slight white drizzle.

"It's Gage," the man said as she craned to see him.

"Oh, great," she muttered to herself.

"I guess you decided not to wait until this afternoon," he said.

"I didn't want to waste time," she said. "I'm going to need a giant can opener to get out."

"Not quite," he said, as he jumped in front of the car. His facial expression no-nonsense, he waved his hand. "Put it in Reverse and don't gun it. Steady pressure," he said.

"Okay," she said and attempted to do what he'd told her. All she did was spin her wheels.

"Okay, now I want you to rock it. Put it in Drive, then Reverse."

She followed his instructions and rocked the car. She was still spinning, but she tried it again and suddenly, the car made several inches backward. "Yay," she cried.

"Good job," Gage said, jumping to the side of the car. "Rock again a couple times then I'm going to give you an extra push.

She followed his instructions. "Reverse," he shouted.

Lissa slammed into Reverse and gunned the pedal while Gage pushed and suddenly she was halfway out of the ditch. "Turn the wheel hard and brake," he said.

The car miraculously didn't slide back into the ditch. Gage tapped on the door. "You ready to get out of there?"

He had no idea, she thought. Lissa released the lock and scrambled from the car so quickly she lost her footing.

"Whoa," Gage said, pulling her to her feet. She felt his brown gaze assessing her and something inside dipped. "You okay?"

She took a deep breath and inhaled the scent of

leather and a hint of cologne. "Of course," she said breathlessly. "I'm just embarrassed and I hate that I probably messed up Melba's car. And I couldn't get out—" She broke off when she realized her words were running together and took another quick breath. "I'm fine."

His lip twitched. "Okay. What I'm gonna do now is pull the car the rest of the way out of the ditch. I tow stuff all the time, so this shouldn't be any different."

Ten minutes later, Gage was pulling the car behind his truck. Lissa sat beside him as he slowly made his way toward the main road.

"I'm sorry I caused you extra trouble," she finally said, glancing at him.

"It happens. It could have been worse," he said with a shrug. "You're lucky you didn't get hurt."

"I really do know how to drive in the snow. I just haven't done as much driving since I've been living in Manhattan," she told him.

"You're just a little rusty. You'll get better with practice. You just might want to take it easy heading out into the snow. We can't be digging you out every day," he said with a chuckle.

"That won't happen," she said a little more sharply than she intended. "I'm not here to cause problems. I'm here to help."

He shot her a quick glance. "Rust Creek Falls

needs that help. You just need to remember you're in a different place. This isn't Manhattan."

"I know that," she said, crossing her arms over her chest.

"Then check the weather and take it seriously the next time you decide to head out into the far parts of the county," he told her.

He was right. She hated it, but he was right. "Will do," she muttered.

"Good. Things will go better that way."

They drove the rest of the way in silence. Gage pulled into the driveway behind the rooming house. Because of all the snow on the vehicle, Lissa wasn't sure how much damage she'd caused. Hopping out of Gage's truck, she rushed to look it over and was shocked to only find a few dents.

"Good grief," she said. "I was sure I totaled it."

Gage walked to stand beside her. "Not Melba's Blue Bomb. It's lasted through floods, blizzards, bumps, wrecks. Everything."

Lissa shook her head. "Do you think Melba will be upset about the scrapes and bumps I left on it?"

Gage chuckled. "She'll be hard-pressed to find 'em. Once you tell her about your little bump with the ditch, she'll be more concerned about your safety than her car."

Melba waddled toward them from the back of the house. "Glory be, thank goodness you're alive," she said, wrapping her arms around Lissa. "I heard all about it from Nanette Gilbert. She heard from Sadie Brown. I think one of the teachers told her when she overheard the conversation with Will. I was sure you would end up in the hospital after such a terrible wreck."

Gage covered a chuckle. "It wasn't all that terrible. She just fell into the ditch and couldn't get out. Everything's okay now."

"Well, you can be sure I'm not going to let you drive if there's any chance of snow. If you'd been hurt, I don't know what I'd do. Come on in and let me give you some soup. You can come, too, if you want, Sheriff."

"That's mighty tempting, Melba, but I've got to get back to the office." He glanced at Lissa. "I'm sure she'll take care of you now."

Lissa met his gaze. "Thank you again for getting me out of the ditch."

He touched his hat. "You're welcome."

Gage walked to his car and drove to his office, the whole time thinking about Lissa and the spark in her eyes. He could tell she felt bad about driving into the ditch. He just hoped like hell she wouldn't do the same thing again. When Will had called him with the news, it had given him a jolt. Will had wanted to go after her, but Gage had insisted, and now he was glad he had. Lissa had been well wedged in that ditch.

Lissa's combination of determination and humility got to him. She had a twinge of pride, but it didn't keep her from going after her goals. She made something inside him rumble and burn, and he didn't like it one bit. He didn't have time for any sort of attraction or distraction.

Frowning, he strode into his office building, where a young blonde woman stood. "What can I do for you?" he asked, trying to place her. "You look familiar, but I don't think we've met. I'm Gage Christensen, the sheriff," he said and extended his hand.

She smiled and accepted his grasp. "I'm Jasmine Cates. I'm from Thunder Canyon. I've been helping my brother-in-law Dean with some construction projects here in town."

"Thank you for your help," he said.

"I'm trying to get in touch with someone by the name of Ann Gilbert. Someone brought some of her furniture in for repair, but the phone number they left is disconnected."

Gage felt a shot of loss. "Some people have left town. The flood was too hard on them. Annie Gilbert fell and broke her hip just after the flood. I think she's been staying in Livingston while she gets back on her feet. I can probably find a way to get in touch with her."

"That would be great," Jasmine said, an expression of relief crossing her face. "Her furniture was beautiful. We really want it returned to her."

"Will do," he said. At that moment, Gary Culbert brought in a casserole dish. "What's up, Gary?"

"Edith made some extra chicken potpie and she wanted you to have it. She really appreciated you helping us get our cattle back last week," the thirty-something-year-old man with a cowlick said. He glanced at Jasmine and tipped his ball cap. "There's more than enough to share."

A moment of silent awkwardness passed and Gage finally met Jasmine's gaze. He shrugged. "You want to join me for dinner?"

She bit her lip. "It's a little early, but…"

"It's early for me, too," Gage said.

"Well, you could heat it up in the microwave," Gary said. "This is good stuff. I appreciate you helping us with the cattle, but I was disappointed when Edith insisted I bring you half of what she was baking."

Gage chuckled. "You sure you don't want to tell her I refused her kind offer so you can take it back home with you?"

"She'd skin me alive," Gary said.

"I can come back in an hour or two," Jasmine said, shoving her hands into her coat pockets.

Gage paused a half beat. *Well, hell.* Maybe Jasmine would keep him from thinking about Lissa.

Jasmine didn't talk as fast as Lissa and she didn't make his gut twist into a knot. "Yeah," he said. "That'll work. I'll see you later, then."

For the next two hours, Gage took care of paperwork, answered calls and touched base with Will. It had been a hell of a day. He raked his hand through his hair as Jasmine walked into the office.

"Rough afternoon?" she asked.

He lifted an eyebrow. "Why do you ask?"

"You don't look—" she smiled "—happy."

"Every day is an adventure," he said, rising to his feet. "Are you ready for that chicken potpie?"

"Sounds good to me," she said.

Gage put the potpie in the microwave and heated it. He pulled out two plates and poured himself a cup a coffee. "We have hot chocolate, coffee and cider. What's your pleasure?" he asked.

"Hot chocolate sounds good for tonight. Thank you," she said.

"Have a seat," he said, motioning toward the chair across from his desk. He spooned the chicken potpie onto the plates and set her plate across from him then served himself. "So, how does Rust Creek Falls compare to Thunder Canyon?"

She chuckled. "Rust Creek is a little more rustic, but the people are great. We have a bit more shopping, but the truth is we still do a lot of shopping online."

"It's nice of the folks from Thunder Canyon to

come and help us," he said and took a bite of the potpie. It was delicious, just as Gary had said.

"We're connected in many ways," Jasmine said. "Why wouldn't we help?"

He nodded and continued the conversation and the meal, but he couldn't keep his mind from wandering to thoughts of Lissa. Damn the woman. Images of her red hair and sparkling eyes slid through his mind. Her determination bumped through him. What was going on, he wondered. This was ridiculous.

Finally, both he and Jasmine had finished the potpie, although he couldn't have recalled much about their conversation if asked.

She stood. "This was fun," she said with a sweet smile.

"Yeah. It was," he said, knowing there wouldn't be a repeat. He couldn't mislead a nice girl like Jasmine until he got Lissa out of his head. He extended his hand to Jasmine. "Thanks for all you're doing for us."

She blinked and shook his hand as if she weren't quite sure how to take him. "Um, you're welcome. Maybe I'll see you again?"

"I'm the sheriff," he said. "Everyone sees me at one time or another."

He sensed her immediate withdrawal and wished he wasn't so distracted by Lissa.

She nodded. "Have a nice night."

Fat chance, he thought.

Lissa leaped off her bed in shock as her alarm sounded the next morning. She still hadn't made the adjustment to Mountain Time. Plus it didn't help that she had driven Melba's car into a snowy ditch yesterday. Even more embarrassing was that Gage had rescued her. She didn't want him to view her as incompetent or a pain in the rear. She hadn't helped her case by going out in the snow yesterday, but she was too impatient to wait to be chauffeured. There was too much to be done.

Taking a quick shower, she pulled on her clothes and sneaked down the back steps. Avoiding the temptation of Melba's full breakfast, she scarfed down a granola bar. The temperature was higher than yesterday, but still cold. She blew into the air and saw her own vapor. In Manhattan, she would have worn a hat, gloves and scarf. Today, she wore the same, but it felt more freakin' freezing. The subway was a lot warmer than the great outdoors of Montana.

She made her way to the mayor's office and was surprised to find it open at such an early hour. Stepping inside, she glanced around and saw an elderly woman focused on paperwork. Although Lissa has never seen the woman, she suspected this was Thelma McGee, the mother of the late mayor.

"Good morning. I'm Lissa Roarke," she said, approaching the counter.

The woman looked up from behind her glasses. "Good morning to you. I'm Thelma McGee."

"I'm honored to meet you," Lissa said.

Thelma's eyes softened. "Thank you. You must know about my son."

"I do," Lissa said. "Everyone talks about what a wonderful man he was."

Thelma sighed. "He was," she said. "And I'm just trying to help keep his office running. But it's not easy."

"Everyone appreciates your effort," Lissa said. "I'm here with the Bootstraps organization to help the town get back on track."

"I can't tell you how much we appreciate your help," Thelma said, rising from the computer. "Rust Creek Falls is a bit remote, so it's hard for us to get enough help. Thank you for coming. We all thank you."

Lissa shrugged. "I'm not sure everyone is all that excited about me being here to help."

Thelma lifted her eyebrows and set a cup of coffee on the counter for Lissa. "Are you talking about Gage?"

Lissa felt a rush of heat rise to her cheeks. "I guess you could say that."

"Gage blames himself for everything. He doesn't understand that he doesn't have the power to prevent a flash flood. He's been through a lot. We all have, but he will come around. It just may take a bit longer." Thelma put her hand over Lissa's. "Give him time. Don't pay attention to his crankiness."

Lissa couldn't help but smile. "I'll work on it. I've heard so many good things about you. Now I understand why."

Thelma waved her hand in dismissal. "Don't flatter me. I just want to honor my son."

Lissa's heart twisted at the woman's words and she felt her determination rise inside her even more strongly. She *would* help Rust Creek Falls. She *would* make a difference.

No matter what Gage Christensen thought about her.

Before he'd had his second cup of coffee, Gage saw Lissa Roarke walk through the door of his office. His stomach rolled. He wasn't ready for this.

"Good morning," she said. "I'm glad you're here. I've thought about the day and I would like to do a little more research on the north side of the county. Do you think you could take me? Or should I ask Will?"

Gage's head was spinning. "Whoa, whoa," he said. "Why do you have to talk so fast? Talking fast isn't going to get anything done faster."

"I just want to get things done as quickly as

possible for your town," she said. "They've been waiting a long time."

"True, but unless you have recruits ready today, there's no need to rush," he said.

Frustrated beyond measure, she barely resisted stomping her foot. "Why are you fighting me on this?" she asked. "Is this personal? Do you dislike what I'm trying to do? If I'm the one who's causing a problem for you, then maybe I should just call my boss and ask for a replacement."

"Why are you jumping off a cliff? I just said you talk way too fast. You just need to slow down," he said.

"You haven't done anything but give me a hard time. Maybe you would be happier with someone else heading up this project," she said.

"You just don't understand what you're getting into. Your degrees may work in New York, but they won't do much here," he said.

"How dare you?" she asked. "I'm just trying to help and all you can do is criticize. You act like I personally made it rain here in Rust Creek Falls. I'm calling my boss so he can have someone else come here to help."

Shaking all over, but trying to hide it, Lissa turned and headed for the door. She reached for it, but Gage's hand covered hers.

"Don't," he said in a low voice.

She glanced back at him and he lowered his

head toward her. He pressed his mouth against hers and her head and heart began to spin. She felt a crazy mix of anger, frustration, desperation and attraction, and her knees buckled from the force of the kiss.

Gage gripped her waist and pulled her against him, his breath heavy. Lissa's stomach dipped. She couldn't remember a time she'd felt like this.

Her gaze clung to his for a long moment. Finally, they both took a breath and she stumbled away from him. She took a deep breath, trying to clear her head.

She couldn't take her eyes from his.

He shook his head and exhaled. "I shouldn't have done that," he said and walked away from her.

Lissa's mind swirled. She locked her knees to keep from falling. She forced herself to pull herself together. How was she supposed to deal with all of this? How was she supposed to conquer her attraction to Gage and help the people of Rust Creek Falls? He'd been prickly enough that she'd been able to resist thinking about him all the time, but she knew there was something under Gage's surface that she found way too compelling. It was more than his cowboy boots and his Stetson. She just couldn't ignore the strength he emanated.

She steeled herself against her feelings. She just had to do it. Nothing, not even Gage Christensen, could or should keep her from her goal.

Lissa kept herself occupied at the desk she'd been given at the sheriff's office with plans for repairs for the next day, but thoughts of Gage plagued her. She had never been kissed like that before. She'd never had such powerful feelings before. Lissa was trying to regain control. She tried to tell herself that Gage hadn't shaken her to her bones, but it was hard.

At the end of the day when she went back to her room, she decided to give her cousin, Maggie, a call. Maggie was a lawyer and was working hard to negotiate a release for Arthur Swinton in Thunder Canyon. Although she was swamped, Maggie answered her cell phone. "How is it going, sweetie?" Maggie asked. "I hope you don't feel like I got you shipped to outer Mongolia."

"No. It's not that bad," Lissa said, laughing at Maggie's reference to the rural nature of where she'd been assigned.

"I hope you don't feel like you got pushed into this, but Rust Creek Falls needed some serious help and I thought you could give it," Maggie said.

"It's okay. Besides, you didn't send me—my boss at Bootstraps sent me. You just used your influence to get Bootstraps involved. I'm glad to be the project coordinator for this job. Plus, you know what they say about cowboys. It's all true. I have to say I have never been so thoroughly kissed,"

Lissa said, giving a big sigh over the kiss she'd shared with Gage.

Maggie chuckled. "Well, congratulations on finding your real-life cowboy."

Lissa rolled her eyes. "No congratulations necessary. This cowboy still acts like he can't stand me."

"What? How can that be?" Maggie asked.

"I can't focus on it. I have a job to do," Lissa said.

"Well, I hope your cowboy will help instead of hinder," Maggie said.

"Me, too," Lissa said. "How's the trial going?"

"Well, they don't call it a trial for no reason," Maggie joked.

Lissa laughed. "Seriously, how's it going?"

"We're making progress," Maggie said. "I'm hopeful."

"Spoken like a true lawyer," Lissa said.

"Yeah, well, that's my job," Maggie said.

"And you do it well," Lissa said.

"Thanks," Maggie said. "Take care, cuz. Call me if you need me."

Lissa sank onto her bed at the rooming house. She definitely felt as if she had bitten off more than she could chew. Dragging her tired body to the bathroom, she washed her face and brushed her teeth then fell into bed. Tomorrow would be a better day.

The next morning, Lissa rose early and indulged in Melba's breakfast—with limits. She spooned her own portions onto her plate instead of letting Melba do it. Afterward, she took a brisk walk toward the sheriff's office. What she really wanted was her own wheels, but after her disaster of driving in the snow, she didn't want to cause any more trouble.

Walking into the office, she heard Gage talking on the phone. She took a deep breath and tried to figure out what to do. She didn't want to interrupt, but she wanted to get to work.

A few seconds later, Gage stopped talking. Lissa chewed the inside of her lip and walked toward Gage's office. She peeked inside. "Hiya," she said.

Gage glanced up at her, his expression clearly displeased. "You're up early."

"So are you. We've both got a job to do," she said.

He nodded reluctantly. "True," he said. "I'll get Will in here. He can take you around this morning."

Lissa felt the chill from five feet away. "Thanks," she said.

"He'll be here in a few," he said.

"Okay. I'll wait in the outer office," she said.

He shrugged. "Not necessary. You can get some coffee and sit anywhere you like. I have to check in with a few people, so I can't give you my undivided attention."

His comment nettled her nerves. "I would never expect your undivided attention," she told him. "I'll sit outside until Will arrives, thank you." *And thank you for being a pain in the butt.*

Chapter Three

Three days later, Gage was still stone-faced when he dealt with Lissa. The good news was that she was getting work done. The mold consultant arrived and conducted evaluations, then taught her how to do the same, which would be more cost-effective as well as a time-saver. She had additional volunteers scheduled to arrive in just a few days.

She shouldn't be giving Gage one more thought, but he was stuck in her mind like a mental burr. She couldn't tell if he was avoiding her because he'd kissed her or because he just couldn't stand her. Neither prospect thrilled her.

Lissa took her regular post-breakfast stroll to the sheriff's office, feeling a little less patient than she had been lately. She usually waited until he'd finished his phone calls, but this time she didn't. She walked right to the door of his office and waved and smiled.

"Good morning, Sheriff," she said in a low voice.

He shot her a considering glance and disconnected his call. "How can I help you, Miss Roarke?"

"I'm actually kind of tired of you helping me. I've respected your advice for several days, but I think I may need to rent an SUV so I won't be such a burden on the sheriff's office," she said.

"You're not a burden," he said. "Will is happy to cart you."

There it was again—the term *cart*. She gritted her teeth. "I'm sure he has other things he needs to do. I'll see if I can get a ride to Livingston to rent a vehicle."

"For my sake and the sake of the entire county, please don't do that," he said, standing.

"I'm not that bad of a driver," she said.

"I have evidence that suggests otherwise," he said in a dry tone.

"I'll have you know that's the only automobile accident I've ever had," she told him.

"Because you usually take cabs or the subway," he said.

"It's not going to snow every day," she argued.

"We'll get some more weather before you know it. Then what will you do?"

"What everyone else does," she said. "Soldier through."

"Sweetheart, trust me on this," he said. "You don't need to be tearing up the back roads of Rust Creek Falls. I don't want to have to rescue you from a ditch or worse."

"One accident and you talk as if I'm completely incompetent," she said. "As if I can't learn how to drive in the snow. You know something, Sheriff Gage Christensen? You are a condescending jerk," she said and walked away.

Fuming all the way back to the rooming house, she climbed the stairs and decided to work from her room today. She could start scheduling the activities of the group of volunteers that would be arriving soon. Sipping hot chocolate, she made calls to the church, where the volunteers would be staying overnight on cots. She double-checked the availability of blankets and linens and was pleased to learn that the community would help prepare some meals for the volunteers.

Lissa contacted the first group of citizens she would be helping. All of them were excited to be receiving assistance. One young mother had been forced to toss all of her children's stuffed animals and favorite comforters due to mold. Lissa added those to the list of things she would do her best to replace.

She skipped lunch, working through it instead, doing her best to avoid thinking about Gage. Oh, how he seemed to know exactly how to upset her and make her feel useless. She would show him. What made it worse was that Gage seemed to be so kind to everyone else. What had she done to make him dislike her so much? *Except for driving into a ditch,* she thought and frowned.

A knock sounded at her bedroom door. "Lissa, this is Melba. You have a visitor."

Curious, Lissa jumped to her feet and swung open the door. "Visitor? Who is it?"

Melba's lip twitched with humor. "Head on down to the front door and you'll find out soon enough."

Lissa followed the older woman down the stairs until Melba stepped aside and waved her hand toward the front door. "Go ahead."

Even more curious now, Lissa opened the door to find Gage standing on the front porch. She stared at him in surprise. "What are you doing here?" she asked.

He gave a wry grin that was somehow too sexy for words. "Now is that any way to greet a guy who brought you flowers?" he asked and presented her with a fistful of flowers he'd hidden behind his back.

Shock and pleasure raced through her. "Wow," she said. "I don't know what to say."

"That's a first," he muttered.

Lissa frowned at him and seriously considered giving back the flowers.

Gage lifted his hands. "Hold on. I'm here to apologize. You're right. I've been acting like a jerk lately."

Lissa dropped her jaw, shocked for the second time.

He sighed. "I haven't been myself since the flood. I shouldn't have—" He cleared his throat. "Kissed you and then taken out my frustration on you. It wasn't fair. If I act like a jerk again, I give you permission to haul off and slug me."

"Oh, I have to confess I've imagined what it would be like to haul off and slug you, but the kiss," she said with a laugh. "The kiss wasn't bad."

He blinked then shot her a smile so charming it took her breath away. "Let's start over. Hi. I'm Sheriff Gage Christensen," he said and extended his hand. "And you are?"

She couldn't resist returning his smile and his handshake. "I'm Lissa Roarke. It's very nice to meet you."

"I'm gonna make sure it's very nice to know you," Gage said.

Lissa felt a funny little twirling sensation in her stomach. "I look forward to that," she said, and she really did.

The next morning, she walked to the sheriff's office and sat at the desk she'd been given in the corner of the front room. She made a list of the calls she planned to make. She was getting excited that the first volunteers would be arriving soon and she could do more than plan. Soon, she would be able to make those promised repairs happen.

A few seconds into her work, a coffee cup and muffin appeared in front of her. She looked up, surprised to find Gage delivering the caffeine and sugar. "Thank you very much. How did I rate this?"

"You're overdue. You rated it before you got here. Though you might not have any room for that muffin if Melba fed you before you left," he said.

"I've learned how to scoot out the back door if I don't want a full country breakfast. Some mornings, it's the most delicious splurge in the world. Other mornings, I don't want that much food."

Gage chuckled. "In my world, I'd love to have that kind of breakfast every day. But maybe not having it's for the best."

Lissa took a big bite of the muffin and chewed on the pastry.

"Looks good," Gage said in approval.

"It is," she said and took another big bite of the muffin.

"Gage," the dispatcher called from across the room. "Harry Leonard's lawn ornaments were stolen again."

Gage groaned. "Somebody needs to give his neighbors' teenage kids something to do. Looks like I may have to be the one. Tell him I'll be right over." He turned back to Lissa. "Let me know if you need anything. Will is escorting a prisoner to Livingston."

"Thanks," she said, trying not to stare too hard at his powerful frame as he left the office. Barely resisting the urge to sigh, she mentally called herself a dork and returned her attention to scheduling repairs.

The dispatcher, Vickie, wandered over to the snack table. "The sheriff is quite the man, isn't he? If I were ten years younger and single, I'd go after him myself. Seems like most of the single girls in town are trying to get his attention. A pretty girl had dinner with him here in the office just the other night."

Lissa felt an unwelcome stab of envy. "He seems so busy all the time. I guess he has to get his companionship when he can."

"Well, I don't know how much companionship is involved. You're right about him being busy. Even though he's on call for the position 24-7, more than one of us wishes he would take a break every now and then. Especially since the flood." The dispatcher shook her head. "He takes it all on himself and can get mighty cranky."

"It must have been hard for him not to be here during the flood."

"Oh, it was," Vickie said. "And losing the mayor... That was a nightmare. The sheriff seems to be sweetening up to you."

Lissa felt a rush of self-consciousness. "I don't think it's personal. I think he values the fact that I'm here to help."

"Hmm. It was nice of him to bring you a little breakfast, though, wasn't it?"

"Yes, it was very nice. But I'm sure he does that kind of thing for everyone. I bet he's done it for you, too," she said.

"Well, maybe if I was slammed with phone calls," Vickie admitted. "But he doesn't look at me the same way he looks at you."

"Up until now, he seemed to look at me like I was a nuisance," Lissa muttered. "I think he's decided I'm determined to help and that's why he's acting nicer."

"You haven't seen the way he looks at you when you're not looking at him. I gotta tell you I think we'd all be happier if the sheriff got a little more—" Vickie broke off and chuckled. "A little more *companionship* on a regular basis. He's a man with needs he's clearly denying. If you can help him out…"

Lissa blinked. Was Vickie suggesting that Lissa take care of his needs? Lissa cleared her throat. "I'm just here to help out with repairs from the flood."

Thank goodness the phone rang, and Lissa was saved from conversation about Gage's needs. She was not, however, saved from a hot image of him, naked and wanting, his eyes burning for her. Lissa felt her body heat all over at the thought. She discreetly fanned herself and decided she could use some cold water.

After a conversation with a very angry Harry Leonard, Gage decided to take a trip to the two neighbors Harry had accused of taking his lawn ornaments. The first was Danielle Hawthorn and her son Buddy. Buddy was fourteen years old and had been involved with some minor looting in the neighborhood. Danielle had two other kids and was raising them by herself since her husband took off three years ago. He'd heard she was working two jobs, so Gage knew she might not be home.

He climbed the steps to the aging house and knocked on the door. Waiting a few seconds, he knocked again. The door opened and Danielle pushed her hair from her face as if she'd just awakened. Her youngest peeked up at him from behind her legs. "Sheriff," she said, her eyes widening in alarm. "Has something happened? Are my kids okay?"

"As far as I know," Gage said. "But you may have a problem. Do you mind if I come inside?"

"No, not at all," she said, opening the door. "Forgive the mess. Tina here is getting over a bad cold."

As if on cue, the little girl sneezed and wiped her nose with the back of her hand.

"That's what tissues are for, sweetie. Go wash your hands real good." She waved her hand toward a chair. "Can I get you some coffee?"

"No. I'm fine, thanks. But I'm a little concerned about Buddy. I got a call from Harry Leonard."

Danielle winced and shook her head. "Oh, no. Not again. I've grounded him too many times to count, but he still finds a way to get together with his friend Jason down the street. They're two peas in a pod and I'm afraid it's turning into a rotten pod. I don't know what to do."

"I have a few suggestions," Gage said. "Seems like Buddy has too much time on his hands, so maybe he could do some volunteering. Does he like any sports? He could help coach some of the elementary kids."

"That's a good idea," she said, then her face fell. "But I'm not always here when he gets home. With my work schedule, I don't know how I could guarantee getting him anywhere after school."

"We might be able to find a way to help you. How about if you talk to Buddy about it?"

Gage visited Jason's family and his parents were similarly appalled. He planned to put Jason in a separate volunteer program. He made a few more visits then headed back to office in the afternoon.

Walking into the office, he saw the dispatcher and Lissa still working at their desks. "Hello, ladies," he said.

"Hi," Vickie said. "I'm headed out in five minutes. It was better than usual today."

"Good," Gage said and turned to Lissa. "How was your day?"

"Good," she said. "I would still benefit from a vehicle."

"As a matter of fact, one of our citizens is willing to donate a truck for your use with the contingency that you don't drive when there's more than a thirty percent chance of snow," he told her.

"I'm grateful for the transportation, but I'm curious how this negotiation took place."

"Harry Leonard has five trucks in his backyard garage and he's willing to let you use one of them, the oldest one."

"Well, Harry sounds like a sweet guy," Lissa said.

"Don't wreck his truck. He'll get cranky," Gage said.

"I'll be careful," she promised, thrilled to have wheels.

"But *no to the snow,*" he told her emphatically.

"Unless you give me a snow-driving refresher course," she said.

"No to the snow," he repeated. "But I'll give you a snow driving course. Just don't test your knowledge."

"Thanks," she said with a huge smile that chipped at his heart. "Whew. It's been a long day. What are you doing now?"

Gage frowned. "Paperwork."

"Bummer," she said and shot him a sideways gaze. "Maybe a pretty girl named Jasmine will keep you company for dinner."

He frowned. "Who told you about Jasmine?"

"Vickie," she said. "She seems to know almost everything."

"Jasmine's a nice young girl working with one of the carpenters," he said.

"Uh-huh," she said. "Nice and attractive. I don't want to keep you from her." Lissa rose from her chair and picked up her iPad.

"No one is keeping me from her. I got a casserole and invited her to have dinner because she was trying to find out how to contact a senior citizen."

Lissa met his gaze for a long moment. "You're a good guy," she said.

"Some people say good guys finish last," he said.

"I wouldn't say that, but I'm headed back to the

rooming house," she said. "I have volunteers arriving tomorrow."

"You seem pleased."

"I'm so excited I can't stand it," she admitted. "We can finally start getting something done."

Her enthusiasm burrowed inside him. He smiled. "Yeah, that's good. And we all appreciate it."

"Thanks," she said. "I'm going to make an early night of it, so I'll be ready to greet the volunteers tomorrow. Thank you for getting me some wheels from Harry Leonard."

"My pleasure," Gage said. "But no—"

"Driving in the snow," she finished for him. "That ditch was no fun for me, either."

"It's dark. You want me to walk you back to the rooming house?" he offered because he wanted to extend his time with her.

"I think I'll be okay," she said. "Rust Creek isn't the most crime-ridden place in the world. But thank you for your chivalry."

Gage gave a rough chuckle. "No one's ever accused me of being chivalrous."

"Well, maybe they haven't been watching closely enough."

Gage felt his gut take a hard dip at her statement. He knew that Lissa was struggling with her visit to Rust Creek and he hadn't made it as easy for her as he should have. There was some kind of electricity or something between them that he couldn't quite name. Just looking at her did something to him.

"I'll take that as a compliment. Call me if you need me," he said.

"Thank you," she said. "Good night."

"Good night," he said and wished she was going home with him to his temporary trailer to keep him warm. Crazy, he told himself. All wrong. She was Manhattan. He was Montana. Big difference. The twain would never meet. Right?

The next day Lissa was so busy she could barely remember her name. Her truck was delivered to her, but she barely drove it because she was busy organizing her first group of volunteers. Gage made a surprise visit at the church.

"I'm Sheriff Gage Christensen," he said to the group. "And I want to thank you for what you're doing for Rust Creek Falls. You may not get a mention on the national news, but you'll be heroes in our hearts forever."

Lissa gave him the heart sign with her fingers pinched together, then shuttled her volunteers toward the vehicles that would transport them. She drove the ancient truck Harry Leonard was allowing her to use. It took some getting used to, but she was thankful to have wheels. The day passed in a flurry of work. The volunteers repaired four houses by the end of the day. Lissa was thrilled. She had estimated three houses, so they were ahead of the game.

She worked nonstop from six in the morning until nine at night every day, making sure the volunteers were well fed and got good rest. By the end of the week she was ready for a long night of rest. She gave her volunteers a recognition banquet provided by the local church and stumbled toward her rooming house.

"Want a beer?" Will asked as he met her on the street.

"I'm too old for a beer," she said with a laugh.

"You're not too old for anything," Will said. "You're hot."

She laughed again. "Not tonight. I just want a good night of sleep. But you're a nice guy to say that. You need to pick someone closer to your age," she said. "You're a great guy."

"You calling me a great guy? That almost makes me feel better that you turned me down," Will said.

"Well, it's the truth. You're a great guy. Don't forget that," she said.

Will tipped his hat. "Thank you very much, Miss Roarke. I'll never think of you as old."

"Thank you for saying that, because I sure am feeling my age tonight." Lissa continued to the rooming house and climbed the stairs to her room.

Tonight she pulled out one of those bottles of red wine and took a swig. She took another sip and wasn't the least bit interested in finishing her glass of wine. Instead she stripped and flung herself into a hot shower. She didn't bother drying her hair, which meant it would be a mad mess in the morning.

Putting a towel on her pillow to absorb the moisture from her hair, Lissa climbed into bed and fell asleep almost immediately. The last image that flew through her mind was of Gage. She could almost feel his arms around her as she drifted off.

Lissa dragged herself out of bed and tried to slide past Melba and her big breakfast the next morning. Melba, however, caught her.

"There you are—our sweet heroine. I've been getting calls all week about what a great job your volunteers are doing. You come sit down and let me give you a good breakfast," Melba said.

"Oh, Melba, that's not necessary," Lissa said.

"Of course, it is. You sit down while I fix you a proper breakfast," Melba said.

Soon enough, a huge platter of eggs, bacon, sausage and pancakes was placed before Lissa.

Lissa bit her lip. "Melba, this is wonderful, but I can't eat all this," she whispered.

Melba's gaze softened. "You don't have to eat it all. My dog, Taffy, will eat anything you don't."

Lissa laughed. "Taffy's getting a bonus meal today, but thank you for being so sweet to me."

"You're the one who's doing so much for us. If you need anything at all, you ask me for it," Melba said.

"Thank you, Melba. You're the best," she said and ate the rest of her eggs and bacon. Who could resist bacon?

She finished her breakfast and went out with the volunteers to the next citizens who needed help with their homes. The day went a bit slower, but it was still productive. She dropped by the sheriff's office before she returned to her room.

"It went well today," she said to Gage.

"So I heard," he said in return.

"Not as fast as the first day, but I'm not complaining," she said.

"Neither am I. I keep getting praise—even from Vickie," he said.

"That's good to hear," she said. "But I'm beat."

"Call me if you need me," he said. "It's supposed to snow tomorrow. I don't want you driving."

"Okay, I won't," she said. "But the church van will be leaving in the morning. I hope we won't have trouble on the roads."

"Check in with me every hour or so," he said.

She nodded. "Okay. Hopefully, the weather

won't prevent us from doing our job. I'm determined."

"I like that about you," he said.

She stared at him for a long moment and wished he would take her in his arms and kiss her. It didn't happen.

"Okay," she said. "I'd like to hear back from you in the morning. Sweet dreams," she said and headed for the door.

"Same to you," Gage said.

Yeah, she thought. The good thing about her sleep tonight was that she was so tired she couldn't avoid it. She couldn't help hoping Gage would struggle with his sleep. Wouldn't it be great if he was tortured by thoughts of her? It would only be fair, she thought.

Very fair.

Chapter Four

What an amazing experience. I've already fallen in love with the people of Rust Creek Falls. The former mayor's elderly mother is determined to continue his legacy by working In the mayor's office. It amazes me the sacrifices the citizens have made in order to stay in Rust Creek and rebuild. Sheriff Gage Christensen is clearly determined to give his all to get the community back on its feet. I'm humbled by all that I'm learning about the people here and the volunteers coming to help.

—Lissa Roarke

Lissa couldn't get Thelma McGee out of her mind, so she bought some flowers from the grocery store and took them to Thelma before she was scheduled to go out with the rest of the volunteers for the day's activities.

"Good morning, Mrs. McGee," she said to the gray-haired woman. "I was thinking about you this morning and wanted you to have these flowers."

Thelma widened her eyes in surprise. "For me?"

"Yes," Lissa said. "For you. You've been working hard. I thought these might brighten up your day."

The older woman fumbled with the blooms. "Well, aren't you a sweetheart," she said.

"You're the sweetheart," Lissa said, correcting her.

Mrs. McGee smiled. "I'm so glad you stopped by. I wanted to invite you to dinner this weekend."

Surprised, Lissa blinked. "Um…"

"Don't say no. I don't invite people to dinner all that often, but I promise the food will be good."

"No doubt it will be," Lissa said. "But you don't have to do this for me."

"It's my pleasure," Mrs. McGee said. "You're so full of life. It makes everyone feel good to be around you. We're blessed that you're here to help us."

Humbled by the woman's kind words. "It will

be my pleasure," Lissa said. "When do you want me to come?"

"Sunday night would be fine. Around six o'clock. Thank you for coming. You've been so good for all of us. I know my son would be so grateful," she said, her voice breaking.

Lissa felt the threat of her own tears. She could only imagine how hard it must be to lose a child at any age. Even an adult child. "I'll be at your house on Sunday night. Thank you for the invitation. I'm honored."

The next three days passed in a blur. By the time Sunday night came around, Lissa was beat, but she was determined to meet her obligation for dinner with Thelma McGee. After the volunteers departed at four, she helped the church strip linens and clean. She took a quick shower before she showed up on Mrs. McGee's front porch at five minutes after six. She felt guilty about those extra five minutes.

Thelma opened the door and beamed at her. "Here you are, our angel. Come on in," she said.

Lissa couldn't remember when she'd been called an angel, but she liked it. It made her want to be even more of an angel. "Thank you, Mrs. McGee."

"Please, call me Thelma," she said and led Lissa through the hallway into a den with plump uphol-stered furniture, soft lamps...and Sheriff Gage Christensen.

He met her gaze with as much surprise as Lissa felt.

"Oh," she said. "Hello."

"Hello to you," he said, holding a glass of something that looked like hard liquor.

"Would you like a cocktail?" Thelma asked. "I gave Gage some whiskey."

"I'm fine," Lissa said, knowing she needed nothing that would make her sleepy. She'd been fighting sleep the entire day.

"Okeydoke," Thelma said. "I'm going to check on my dinner."

Silence followed as she left.

"What are you doing here?" Gage finally asked before he knocked back his whiskey.

"She invited me a few days ago. I tried to refuse, but—"

Gage shook his head. "No one can refuse Thelma. Especially now."

"So what are you doing here?"

"I come every other week. I know she's lonely, and with her son gone…"

He looked at his glass as if he were wishing for more whiskey.

"Well, hey, we repaired some more houses today," she said cheerfully.

"That's good news."

"Another crew is coming next week," she said.

"Gotta give it you, you're pulling in a lot of help. We're really grateful," he said.

"It's what I do," she said. "Just like being a sheriff is what you do."

He paused then nodded and took one last sip from his squat glass. "Yeah."

That one word was just too sexy. If anyone else had said it, it wouldn't have affected her, but when Gage looked at her that certain way and said *yeah,* something inside her quickened and shifted.

Thelma returned with a smile and clasped her hands together. "Dinner is ready."

Grateful for the distraction, Lissa focused her attention on Thelma. "Perfect," she said. "I can't wait."

Lissa did the best acting job she could ever remember. She focused on Thelma and her pot roast and vegetables. She enjoyed the sweet potatoes added to the traditional mixture.

"I cook it all in the oven, covered and at a low temperature for a long time. That's the secret. Low temperature, and don't rush," Thelma said. "Everyone is in such a rush these days, cooking everything in a microwave. If you're not careful, your dinner will taste like cardboard."

Lissa nodded and spared a quick glance at Gage. "I can't deny what you're saying. When I'm in New York, I either heat something up in the microwave or order takeout."

Thelma laughed. "The only takeout we have here is when a friend delivers a meal."

"I get a lot of those," Gage said. "I'm lucky, though. Just like tonight with your pot roast I'm a charity case."

Thelma laughed again. "You're anything but a charity case. The old women are grateful to you. The young women want a date with you."

"And in between?" Gage asked as he took another bite of pot roast.

"In between, they want you to help with their kids. Tell me I'm wrong," Thelma said.

Gage shook his head. "Can't say you're wrong. You're a smart woman, Mrs. McGee."

"I keep asking you to call me Thelma so I'll feel younger," she said with a coy smile. "Well, I must make a toast," she said, lifting her still-full glass of wine. "To Gage, for working too much to help Rust Creek Falls recover. And to Lissa, for giving us the spark we needed to make our community better. I am so grateful to both of you, just as my son would have been."

Lissa lifted her water glass as Gage lifted his. "Cheers," she said along with him and saw the pain in his eyes.

An hour later, Lissa saw that Mrs. McGee was fading. Lissa covered a yawn. "Oh, my goodness, I'm so tired. You're putting me to shame. Your dinner filled me up and made me want to go to sleep."

Thelma caught her yawn and covered her mouth. "You've been working hard. Having both of you here tonight has been so wonderful."

"Oh, no," Lissa said. "This has been a huge treat for me."

"And for me," Gage added. "I would have had muffins and a burger for dinner if not for this. And trust me, your company was much better than my own."

Thelma sighed. "Well, we're all connected by our love for this community. I'm so grateful for both of you."

"We are grateful for you," Gage said. "Now let us help clean up, or both Lissa and I will be offended."

"Well, now, I wouldn't want to offend you," Thelma said.

Lissa and Gage cleaned up the dishes in a short time, chatting all the time with Mrs. McGee as she sat in a chair in the kitchen. They both said their goodbyes and thank-yous to the lovely woman and walked out the door.

On the porch, she looked up at Gage. "She's a great woman."

"Yeah, and she had a great son," he said, his gaze sad.

"She seemed happy," Lissa said, inhaling the cold night air.

Gage nodded. "I can drive you home," he said.

"It's not that far," she said. "I can walk."

"I'll drive," he insisted and escorted her to his SUV. He opened the door to the passenger side and helped her into her seat then rounded the car to the driver's seat.

He pulled away from the curb.

"How was your day?" she asked.

"Could have been worse. I'm a little concerned about some drug dealers coming into my territory," he said.

"Oh, no," she said, staring at him.

"Plenty of dealers and manufacturers try to move into rural territories, but I've been pretty good about keeping them away. It takes some extra effort. I'll get some help from the state and get them gone."

"That's good. I would have thought drug dealers would be the last thing you would find in Montana," she said.

"Meth users are everywhere. They're like cockroaches. It's my job to stamp them out here, to make it difficult to survive and thrive. So far, I've been successful," he said.

"I'm glad to hear that," she said.

"It's kind of crazy," he said. "More than half of my time is spent on nothing serious. Lawn ornaments and other stuff. I won't tolerate drugs."

"Your community is lucky they have you and

that you have your attitude. You're very protective," she said. "You're an excellent sheriff."

His lips lifted in a slow, sexy smile. "Thanks, Lissa."

Lissa felt a crazy dip in her belly and leaned toward him. "Yes," she said, wanting him to meet her halfway with a kiss that would knock her into next week. "Yes."

A long silence followed. Gage cleared his throat. "Uh, we're here. I can walk you to the front door of the rooming house."

Lissa gaped outside the window of his SUV, surprised to see the rooming house. She tried to gather her wits. "Oh, that's not necessary. Thanks for the ride home," she said and tried to get out of the car. Without unlocking the door first. Finally, she remembered to unlock and push open the door, sliding out onto the ground.

"Good night," she said, determined not to look at him.

"Hey, Lissa," he said.

She couldn't help but turn back around to look at him. "Yes?"

"Thank you for what Bootstraps is doing for us. You're making a big difference," he said.

She gave a slow nod, her mind fighting with her hormones. "You're welcome," she managed, and climbed the steps to the rooming house. She made her way to her room and kicked off her boots.

Totally exasperated, she frowned and scowled at Gage's reaction to her.

Gratitude, she thought. She didn't want gratitude. She wanted passion. Stripping off her clothes, she took a quick shower and pulled on comfy pajamas, cursing Gage all the time. She impulsively poured herself a tiny glass of red wine and took a gulp. Shrugging, she poured the wine down the drain. She wanted cold, cold water instead, and drank some down.

"Could be worse," she said and told herself to get a good night's sleep. "Tomorrow will be ten times better."

She slumped back against her pillow and pulled the covers over her. "When I wake up in the morning, I'm not going to want Gage Christensen. I'm not going to think of Gage Christensen. I'm going to purge him from my system while I sleep."

She kept repeating those words until she fell asleep.

When Lissa awakened in the morning, her first thought was of Gage.

Gage woke up with an uncomfortable jangly sensation inside him. Maybe he should fix his house, so he could make it a home again. The only problem was that he didn't have time. He couldn't see fixing his own house before other people's homes that needed far more work.

He felt grungy and his back was sore. As much as he told himself that the new sofa bed didn't affect his back, he was so wrong. Maybe he was getting old, he thought, as he stumbled to his feet and into the shower. Shoving himself under the shower, he lifted his face to the spray. He would have fallen asleep a lot sooner last night if he hadn't been thinking about Lissa. He didn't want to be thinking about Lissa. He didn't want to be feeling anything for Lissa.

He scowled, focusing on the shower, willing it to clean out his head. He spent some extra moments under the spray then dragged himself out of it and scrubbed himself dry. Gage got dressed and walked out to his car, his mind filled with too many people. The former mayor, his mother and Lissa.

Swearing under his breath, he was determined to extricate his distractions from his head. He turned his favorite country station on super loud and drove toward the office.

He walked inside to find the dispatcher already at her desk. "Mornin', Vickie. How are you?"

"I'm awake and drinking my second cup of coffee, so that's pretty good. How are you?" she asked.

"I've only had one cup, so I better catch up with you," he said with a wink and poured himself a cup. At that moment, Will walked into the office. Gage gave his deputy a nod of greeting.

"I got a call from Danielle," said Vickie. "She said something about her son doing some volunteer work, but said she's going to need some help with transportation."

"Right," he said. "I'm wondering if we can expand the volunteer elder care drivers to anyone else who might need transportation if they have a good reason."

Will snickered. "I don't think Harry Leonard is going to want to transport his juvenile neighbors anywhere except the moon."

Gage swallowed a chuckle. "Can't deny that, but I think we need to keep some of these teens busy before they get into real trouble."

Will sobered. "True. I'm in."

"You're already in over your head," Gage said. "But I appreciate your commitment. I'll put out a request for some volunteers. In the meantime, you and I may be doing some extra carting."

"We've doing a lot of that with Lissa here, at least before Harry loaned her a truck," Will said. "Not that I minded. She's so hot."

Gage felt a trickle of irritation. "Back down, hound dog. You're too young for her, anyway."

Will stiffened his spine and stuck out his chin. "That's a matter of opinion. She seems to respect me."

"Lissa respects everybody," Gage said, growing more irritated by the second.

"She sure does," Vickie said. "But I've noticed more than one man giving her the eye. I wouldn't be surprised if somebody didn't try to snap her up."

Gage frowned. "What do you mean somebody will snap her up? She's too busy for that."

Vickie shrugged. "Everyone has a weak moment and Lissa is a beautiful woman…."

Will cleared his throat. "Well, I'm ready anytime she wants a ride."

Gage ground his teeth. "Step back, deputy," he said and headed for his desk. *What a rotten start to the day.*

"On another subject, I also heard that the Crawfords are spreading rumors about your brother-in-law, Collin," Vickie said in a low voice.

"What do you mean?" he asked, wondering what other bad news he was going to get.

"Those Crawfords are determined that Nate win the post as mayor. They don't think Collin Traub deserves to be mayor, and I'm afraid they may turn this into a dirty race. Everyone should be prepared for it."

Gage sighed. "Thanks for letting me know," he said and made a mental note to talk to Collin. It was always best to be prepared.

A call came in and Gage hit the ground running.

A robbery followed by a fire followed by someone who needed an appendectomy. He also checked by the abandoned house where he'd discovered an illegal drug manufacturer doing business a month ago to make sure no one else had set up shop there. By the end of today he was ready for a trip to Jamaica. But he knew that wouldn't happen. He finally walked back into his office, late. Very late.

The late dispatcher had arrived and was asleep at the desk. Gage couldn't blame the poor guy. Thank goodness there usually weren't many calls at night. Sighing, he walked toward his office.

He heard a soft feminine voice. "Enough for the day," she murmured.

He knew that voice. Lissa. He headed toward her little corner. "How's it going?"

"Long day," she said. "I made a few home visits and a lot of calls. I want to make sure everything is ready for our next group of volunteers."

Gage nodded. "Sounds like you're on top of it.

She rolled her eyes. "That's relative."

He chuckled. "Give me a minute and I'll give you a ride to the rooming house."

She waved her hand. "No need."

"Give me a minute," he told her and went to his office and collected his messages. Thank goodness, nothing was an emergency.

He returned just as Lissa headed out the door.

"Hey," he called, running after her. "Why didn't you wait?"

She glanced back at him. "You've got enough to do. I don't want you to feel like you have to look after me."

"I was just going to drive you back to the rooming house," he said.

She shoved her hands into her pockets. "I can walk. It's not that far or I would use the truck Harry Leonard is letting me use. But actually a couple people invited me to the bar. I thought I might stop there before I headed back to my room."

Surprise rolled through him. "I haven't heard you talk about going to the bar since you've been here."

She shrugged. "I hear change can be good."

He gave a slow nod. "Yeah. I'll take you to the bar," he said, feeling overly protective, but determined not to show it.

"Okay, thanks," she said with a smile.

He helped her into his SUV and drove to the bar, parking in a spot several spots away from the door. Escorting her out of the car, he walked inside the bar with her. Loud country music was playing and the place was filled with the smell of beer and hard liquor. A few couples shuffled around on the tiny dance floor. The smell of tobacco permeated the bar even though patrons were required to smoke outside.

"Is this working for you?" he asked. "Just like a Manhattan bar, right?"

She knitted her brows together. "It's a bit primitive, but it could be worse. I'm going to be here awhile longer, so maybe I should respect the native culture." She glanced up at him and shot him a sassy smile.

His gut took a twist and turn. "If you say so. What would you like to drink?"

"I'm betting they can't make a cosmopolitan or appletini," she said with a sigh.

"I think you're betting right."

"Okay. I'll take vodka and orange juice. That can't be too hard."

Gage tipped his hat. "I'll see what I can do," and he went to the bar. "I'll take a vodka and orange juice and a beer for me."

The bartender gave him a second look. "Vodka and orange juice. I don't think we have any orange juice."

"Do you have any fruit juice?" Gage asked.

The bartender searched his inventory. "We've got some lime."

Gage rubbed his face. "Put in a lot of lime and anything else sweet you have."

"Sweet," the bartender echoed. "We may have some grenadine in the back, for wimps."

"This is for a wimp," Gage said. "A woman wimp."

"Oh," the bartender said. "Why didn't you tell me that from the beginning?" The bartender left, poured the drinks and returned to give them to Gage. "She'll like this," he said.

"What makes you so sure?" he asked.

"Trust me," the bartender said. "I've never had any complaints."

Gage swallowed a sip of his beer and took the drink to Lissa. She accepted it and took a swallow. "Yum," she said. "This is good."

"Take your time," he said.

"Oh, look, it's Jared and Will. They've both been trying to get me to come here. Let's go visit them," she said.

Gage caught sight of the two men she'd mentioned. One was his deputy. The other was the Romeo of Rust Creek Falls. He wondered how in the world Jared Winfree had gotten to Lissa.

Although he didn't respond, he escorted her toward Jared and Will. Both men looked hesitant at his presence.

"Howdy," he said to Jared and Will and took another sip of beer.

"Howdy," Jared said then turned to Lissa. "Are you having a good time?"

She smiled. "I'm working on it. It sure is loud here."

Will nodded. "Yeah, they try to make it feel like a party every night. You wanna dance?"

She blinked. "I think I just want to soak up the atmosphere," she said.

Jared moved closer to her. "I bet you don't have this kind of bar in Manhattan," he said.

Lissa glanced down at the peanut shells on the floor and nodded. "Not that I've seen. But I haven't been to every bar in the city."

Jared slid his arm on the bar behind her back and Gage felt an unwelcome itchy feeling up and down his spine.

"So, how did we get so lucky to have you come to Rust Creek Falls?" he asked.

Lissa looked vaguely uncomfortable. "One of my cousins and I wanted to try to help after the flood. It took a bit of persuading, but my boss finally thought it was a good idea."

Gage cleared his throat. "Where are you from, Jared?"

Jared touched his hat. "I've been in Rust Creek since the flood because the work is here. Before that I've been a rambling kind of man."

"Yeah, so where were you born?" Gage asked.

Jared shrugged. "Doesn't matter where you're born. It's where you've lived that makes you. Right, Lissa?"

"I've lived most of my life in upstate New York and spent the past several years in the city, so I can't comment. I will say that Manhattan is a different world compared to most of the rest of the country," she said.

"Exactly," he said, pointing at her. "Exactly."

Gage found Jared's flirting irritating, but he wasn't going to waste his energy commenting. Instead, he took another long drink of beer.

"So, how do like to spend your spare time?" Jared said, crowding Lissa even more.

She wiggled a little as if she were trying to create some space for herself, but Jared didn't give an inch. "I haven't had a lot of spare time since I got here," Lissa said. "What do you like to do in your spare time?"

"Well, I like this bar and I like pretty, smart girls. You sure I can't talk you into dancing with me?" he asked, leaning in toward her.

It was all Gage could do to keep from jerking Jared out of her range.

Lissa took a deep breath and another sip of her drink. "Like I said, I'm just trying to soak up the atmosphere."

"Let me get you another drink," Jared said and turned toward the bartender.

"Oh, no. I don't need—"

"Sure you do. Every night is Friday night here," Jared said.

"But…"

A young man approached Lissa. "You're the pretty new girl in town. I'm David and I'm here to welcome you to Rust Creek Falls," he said. "Come on and dance with me."

"Oh, no…"

"Now, don't be shy," he said, taking her hand and nearly dragging her onto the dance floor.

Both Jared and Will stared and frowned.

"Who the hell was that?" Will asked.

"Some guy named David who got Lissa on the dance floor," Gage said.

Jared swore under his breath. "Well, that's not gonna happen."

"Whoa," Gage said, but Jared was clearly determined. He stalked onto the dance floor and confronted David.

Gage shook his head, getting a bad feeling in his gut. "This doesn't look good."

"Damn straight," Will said. "How'd this no-name get Lissa to dance with him?"

"Rein it in, cowboy," Gage said. "You're a lawman first."

One second later, Jared took a swing at David. After that, all hell broke loose. Gage soldiered through the crowd, dodging several punches. He found Lissa sitting on the floor, looking dazed and frightened.

"Come on," he said, extending his hand to her.

Taking his hand, she rose. "What in the world—"

"It doesn't take much for some guys to get riled

up. Stay close," He moved through the crowd, again dodging punches. "I'm going to get you to the rooming house, then I'll come back here to settle all this down."

"I can walk by myself," she said.

"Hell, no. You've caused enough trouble. The next thing I know you'll be inciting a riot in the streets."

"I wouldn't incite anything," she complained.

Gage lifted a dark eyebrow. "I think you underestimate your effect on men."

Chapter Five

The next morning, Lissa was extremely reluctant to go to her so-called *command central* at the sheriff's office. She'd heard enough from Melba at breakfast this morning. Everyone was buzzing about the fight at the bar last night. Melba wanted to know which guy Lissa was favoring since several had tried to get her attention. Lissa just asked for more bacon.

After dawdling an extra fifteen minutes, she walked to the sheriff's office and braced herself.

"Well, hello to you Miss Bachelorette," Vickie said.

Lissa winced. "Maybe I should work from the rooming house."

"No, no," Vickie said, moving toward her with a chocolate-chip muffin. "We got extra treats this morning due to you. Don't you go anywhere," she said.

Lissa lifted her hand in refusal. "I just stuffed myself with a breakfast from Melba. I don't know when I'll eat again."

"She's a good cook," Vickie said. "I hear both Gage and Will got socked in the face," she said in a lowered voice. "I can't wait to see if either of them got a black eye."

Lissa bit her lip. "Don't tell me that. I just thought it would be fun to visit the local bar."

Vickie chuckled. "You gave a lot of us a good time."

"But not Gage and Will," she muttered.

"They got a different kind of excitement," Vickie said. "Oh, darn. There's the phone."

The door flung open and Will walked in, wearing a pair of sunglasses. "Hey," he said to Lissa and walked past her.

Lissa winced, wondering what was behind those glasses. "Hi, Will," she said. "How are you?"

"We had to arrest two people last night. We locked the rest of them in a barn for the night," he said.

"I'm so sorry," she said.

"Yeah, it makes for a lot of paperwork," he said and disappeared into his cubicle.

Lissa grabbed a cup of coffee and sat down at her desk. Her concentration nil, she pulled up her list for the day. "Corwin," she said. "I need to call the Corwins to make sure they're ready for repairs."

A moment later, Gage strode through the door, his left cheek red and swollen. He wasn't hiding it. "Hey," he said to Lissa. "Got paperwork."

"Yeah, that's what Will said," she said.

Lissa stared after him, feeling extremely guilty. She hated that she had caused extra work for Gage again. First, falling in a ditch. Second, going to a bar—the only bar in Rust Creek Falls—and starting a fight. Lissa frowned. She wasn't a knockout. How had this happened?

After staying sequestered in his office for several hours, Gage headed out to conduct a patrol and make a few calls. Lissa worked through the day, but was terribly distracted. Finally, at five o'clock, Gage returned to the office. "Hey, Vickie. Give me the most important messages," he said.

"Good news," she said, giving him a couple sheets of paper. "Nothing major."

He flipped through them and nodded. "I'll make some return calls and plan on some visits tomorrow."

"When do you ever get your ranching done?" she asked.

"We have a few people helping out," he said. "I try to handle the morning chores."

"Bet you'd like to sleep late one of these days," she said.

"Yeah," Gage said. "One of these days."

"Well, I'm headed out," she said. "Good night to you and Miss Lissa."

"Good night, Vickie," Lissa called.

Gage echoed her words. Lissa approached him. "I'm sorry about what happened last night. I had no idea my dancing with someone would cause such a problem."

"Yeah, well, this is Montana. Not New York," he said.

His response stabbed at her. "Are you saying dancing causes issues in Montana?"

"A beautiful woman causes issues anywhere," Gage said.

"I'm not that beautiful," she retorted.

Gage looked at her in disbelief. "That's a matter of opinion. Just do me a favor and stay away from the bar for the next few days. I don't have the manpower to handle hot crazy men acting out around you."

"Are you saying this is my fault?"

"I'm saying you underestimated yourself," he said.

She scowled at him. "That's ridiculous. You act as if I can exert control over whoever I encounter."

"Well, here's a news flash. I haven't had to

make arrests at the bar for two months. I don't have time for this, so do me a favor and skip the bar. If you want a martini, I'll buy it for you and deliver it to the rooming house."

Lissa felt her frustration build inside her like a bomb ready to explode. Her whole body roared with heat. "You're being a jerk. A complete jerk," she told him, her voice getting louder with each syllable. She stepped close to him, lifted her chin and poked her finger against his hard chest repeatedly. "If you think I'm so beautiful, why don't you stop being such an idiot and kiss me?"

Complete silence followed, but Lissa didn't break eye contact with Gage. She didn't even blink.

But he did and he took a long breath. "Do you realize you just asked me to kiss you?"

"Well, somebody needs to do something about this insanity," she said.

Gage stared at her for a long moment then began to chuckle. "Darlin', I thought you'd never ask," he said and pulled her against him and took her mouth in a kiss that made the room turn upside down. Her heart hammered against her rib cage, her breath stopped in her throat and her blood raced through her veins like wildfire. The kiss seemed to scream his need and desire for her.

The power of it made her knees weak. She clung to his shoulders, wanting to get closer to him, much closer. Lissa could feel the evidence of his arousal pressed against her. He lifted one of his hands to her jaw, tilting her mouth to give him better access. The move only made her more aroused.

"Oh, Gage," she whispered. "I want you so much." She rubbed herself against him, resenting the clothes between them.

He slid his hand down to one of her breasts and she immediately felt her nipple harden against her bra. She tugged at his jacket and somehow opened it.

He made a growling sound that rumbled through her like the threat of a powerful thunderstorm. There was a sense of inevitability and anticipation that wrapped around them like a cord, drawing tighter and tighter.

Gage pulled back, swearing under his breath, his eyes as dark as midnight. "There's only one way this is going to go tonight, and I'm not making love to you in the office. Come to my place?"

"Yes," she said, because her mouth, her body, her heart wouldn't let her say anything else. So caught up in her feelings for him, she almost walked out the door without her jacket.

"Hey, hold on there," Gage said, grabbing the coat for her. "I don't want you getting chilly on the way."

She laughed. "I don't think there's much chance of that."

Gage locked up the office and escorted her to his SUV. He started the engine and glanced at her. "You sure about this?"

"I've never been more sure," she said.

Groaning, he leaned toward and took her mouth in a long, hot kiss. He pulled back and shook his head. "Can't remember feeling this way," he muttered and drove toward his property.

After a moment of silence, he reached for her hand. "I better warn you my temporary trailer isn't five-star," he told her.

"I'm not worried about the accommodations. I just want the man," she said.

"You know the right thing to say to make a man feel good, Lissa," he said.

She just hoped she knew all the other things that would make him feel good. She wasn't particularly experienced....

Soon enough, he turned onto a dirt road. "I take care of this part of the ranch. My parents handle the other. It's big enough that between being sheriff and doing my chores here I can go weeks without seeing them," he said.

"I imagine they don't like that," she said.

He shrugged. "Everyone knew I would have less time for ranching once I was elected sheriff. I had to be talked into running. It was one of those jobs that chose me."

"Do you wish you hadn't run for office?" she

asked, because he seemed such a natural for the position.

"It's turned into one of those things that seems like it was meant to be. That doesn't mean there aren't tough situations or tough days, but I like being part of the solution." He stopped in front of a trailer and a darkened house.

"I bet you wish you could get back into your house," she said.

"It's not on the agenda at the moment," he said. "There are too many people in worse shape than I am."

"Spoken like a true self-sacrificing community servant," she said and leaned toward him. "But you don't have to sacrifice every moment to the job, do you?"

His eyes lit with arousal. "Not with you around," he muttered and got out of the car. He walked to her side of the vehicle, opened the door and extended his hand. Her stomach dipped as she accepted his strong grip and slid out of the SUV.

She barely took two steps before he swung her up in his arms.

Surprised, she gazed up into his face. "What's this?"

"I just thought you should see that we do things a little different than your Manhattan boys," he said.

"Oh," she said. "Are you saying all the Montana men do this?"

He shot her a mock scolding glance. "Now don't get any ideas."

She shook her head. "Too late. You give me a lot of ideas."

"Just as long as they're about me," he said and set her down when he reached the door.

Leading her into the small trailer, he flipped on a light and turned to her. "I warned you it's not fancy," he told her.

"You also told me you do things different than those Manhattan boys," she said, poking her finger at his chest. "When are you going to show me?"

He grinned. "I think now is good," he said and pulled off his jacket.

Her heart started to hammer when he pulled off her jacket, too. "Come here, darlin'," he said and pulled her into his arms.

He felt so good. All muscle and male, he lowered his mouth to hers in a long, deep kiss that rattled her down to her toes.

He took her by surprise by swinging her into his arms as he walked into a small bedroom. She would never have believed how feminine and desirable that made her feel. Lissa lifted her hands to his face, relishing the slight abrasion of his barely whiskered jaw. Everything about him felt like a *man* to her: the coiled strength of his muscles, his wide shoulders and the way his large hands wrapped around her.

He let her slide down his body, keeping her so close she felt every nuance of him. He kissed her again and she followed her body and mind's instinct, pulling his shirt loose from his jeans. She slid her hands up his bare torso and he sucked in a sharp breath.

"You're making it hard for me to move slow," he said.

"Maybe I don't want you to move slow. I swear I feel like I've been waiting for you to kiss me forever."

"Well, I'm gonna be doing a lot more than kissing you," he said, and pulled her sweater over her head. A half breath later, her bra was gone and he was putting her down on the bed. Following her down, he slid his mouth down her throat to her nipples. Her body felt as if it were on fire. He caressed her until she couldn't remain still any longer.

"Gage," she said, asking, wanting more.

His skin was warm beneath her touch. She skimmed her hands down over his abdomen and unbuttoned his jeans. When she touched him where he was hard and needing her, he swore under his breath.

He took her mouth again and within moments, they pushed each other's clothes away. Her heart raced and she could barely catch her breath. Lissa had never wanted a man so much in her life. Yes, he was incredibly sexy, but he was smart and funny —nearly perfect.

When he caressed her intimately, her mind seemed to stop. "Gage," she pleaded.

"Hold on," he said and pushed her legs apart. His gaze holding hers, he thrust inside her, filling her with him. She clung to him as he moved in a delicious rhythm that made her feel as if everything inside her was tightening with his every stroke. He reached between them and caressed her once again, and Lissa felt herself burst over the edge.

Seconds later, she felt him stiffen and groan as he climaxed.

Lissa knew she would never be the same.

It took Gage fifteen minutes to make the muscles in his legs start working. This little city gal had knocked him sideways. Granted, it had been a while since he'd been with a woman, but he couldn't remember anyone making him this hot and bothered then utterly depleted.

She looked so pretty in his bed with her hair spilled over his pillow, her lips swollen from him kissing her. He looked down at her naked body and felt the urge to take her again. Well, hell, he didn't want her to think he was a complete animal.

Turning his head aside to get a little control, he scrubbed his jaw. "You hungry?" he asked.

Silence followed. "Uh, I hadn't been thinking about food, but now that you mention it I guess I am."

He felt her soft hand on his shoulder and shuddered. She hesitated. "You don't like that?" she asked.

He chuckled then took her hand and pressed it against his mouth. "Too much. It's not gourmet, but how about a grilled cheese sandwich and some soup?"

"Sounds perfect to me," she said, smiling at him.

Gage took one last glance at her tempting naked form and rose from the bed. He pulled a flannel shirt from his drawer and tossed it at her. "Here, cover up. I don't want you getting cold."

"You got me pretty warm without a shirt a few minutes ago," she said in a sexy teasing voice.

"Maybe I'll get you warm again after I feed you. I don't want to be accused of torture," he said.

"If that was torture…" she drawled.

"Put on the shirt, Lissa," he said and pulled on his jeans. "You are too much."

Gage fixed three sandwiches and a can of tomato soup. He offered her a beer, but she asked for water. "Sorry I don't have wine," he said.

"That's okay. You can pick some up for next time," she said with a smile.

"So there's gonna be a next time?" he asked,

liking the idea. At the same time, he knew Lissa was only in town for a short time and he knew he shouldn't get attached to her.

"Do you want to go back to just being friends? No kisses. No touching. No anything," she said, then took a big bite of the sandwich and gave a little moan of approval.

Hell, no, he thought. "You make a good point. I guess we just both need to remember that you're not going to be here forever. So this is temporary."

A shot of vulnerability deepened her eyes for a half second before she looked away. It happened so fast he wondered if he had imagined it. "You're so right," she said, then met his gaze. "This is temporary, so we should make the best of it, shouldn't we?"

Her eyes seemed to challenge him to all sorts of things he'd never imagined. Gage nodded, feeling him sink under her spell. "Yeah, we should."

"So, next time you'll have wine for me, right?" she asked with a smile.

"Sure. White, red or pink?" he asked.

"White," she told him. "Tell me, are you going to take me home tonight or keep me here with you?"

"That's easy," he said. "I'm keeping you here with me."

After a crazy night of lovemaking, Gage and Lissa took a shower together. She dressed in the clothes she'd worn yesterday. He dressed in fresh clothes and they headed for town. "I'll drop you off at the rooming house, okay?"

"That works for me. I have one more day before my next group of volunteers arrive."

"And we'll keep this on the down low, right?"

He felt her gaze on him. "Are you ashamed of being involved with me?"

He glanced at her. "Hell, no. I wanted to protect your reputation."

She widened her eyes. "Hadn't thought of that." She paused for a moment. "I guess if someone's going to ruin my reputation, I'd like it to be you."

"Well, I'm flattered. But if there's a way to protect you, I'll take it," he said.

Again, he felt her admiring gaze on him. "What?" he asked.

"You're pretty amazing," she said.

Her words made him warm and feel good inside. "Not really, but I'll take the compliment," he said.

As Gage stopped next to the rooming house, Lissa leaned toward him and took his mouth in a scorching kiss that reminded him of all they'd done the night before.

"Have a nice day, Sheriff," she said when she finally pulled away.

His whole body on fire, he wondered when he'd be able to rein in his sex drive for her. He needed to get it under control, he thought as he watched her take the steps to the rooming house. When she disappeared inside, he drove to the office and strode into complete quiet. Thank goodness.

He went to his office and began to work on messages and paperwork from the previous day. He heard someone enter the office, but continued working. Moments later, Vickie poked her head in his office with a cup of coffee in her hand.

"I hear the sheriff had a nice visit with our new favorite gal, Lissa Roarke," she said and put the cup of coffee on his desk.

"Wouldn't know," he said.

"Well, everyone else does," she said. "Did you really think Melba would keep it quiet when Lissa didn't come back last night?"

"Like I said," he repeated firmly. "I wouldn't know."

Vickie made a huffing sound of disapproval. "It will go easier if you go ahead and admit that you two are involved. But I can tell you're determined to take the hard way. Good luck."

Gage glanced up after Vickie left. He sure as hell hoped the whole town didn't know about his involvement with Lissa after just one night. How could he protect them both against such public study?

The phone rang, taking his focus from the possibility of the scrutiny. It was another drug call that would consume him for the rest of the day. Gage would do just about anything to keep drugs out of Rust Creek.

Lissa took her time putting on fresh jeans and a sweater. She tiptoed down the back stairs with the intent of sneaking out the back door. Melba's voice stopped her.

"Hey there, darlin'. I hear you've been visiting with Gage," the woman said.

Lissa froze, turning back to meet Melba's gaze. "Maybe a little," she said, not wanting to reveal too much.

Melba folded her hands together. "Well, I must tell you that the whole community of Rust Creek Falls is grateful."

Lissa felt her cheeks flush with heat. "Uh, you're welcome."

"Yes, indeed," Melba said. "We are very thankful. Gage is the best sheriff we've ever had. We want him happy, and it looks like you help keep him that way."

Lissa blinked. "I'm not sure…"

"No need to be sure about anything. We're just glad you're here, making our town better and making Gage happy. Anything I can get for you? I know it's late for breakfast, but I'm happy to make something for you."

"I'm good," she said. "Thanks, Melba."

Lissa scurried out the door into the cold air of near autumn in Montana and prayed the rest of Rust Creek Falls didn't know about her and Gage. She could only hope.

Something told her to take it slow as she walked to the sheriff's office. She entered with a light step. No need to stomp. Heading for her little corner desk, she waved at Vickie, but kept moving. She made it to her desk with no confrontation and took a deep breath.

Seconds later, Vickie stepped in front of her desk. "Hey there, sweetie. I hear you had a nice time last night."

Lissa straightened in her chair. "What makes you say that?"

Vickie blinked. "Well, people are saying that you and Gage…"

"What people?" Lissa asked. "What are they saying? What do they really know?" she asked.

Vickie opened her mouth, but no sound came out. "Uh…"

"Exactly," Lissa said. "Nobody knows anything. This is personal."

Vickie's eyes widened. "Uh…"

"Uh," Lissa said. "Exactly. And I thank you so much for respecting that because you have been a friend to me ever since I arrived in Rust Creek Falls."

Vickie stared at her for a long moment then gave a slow nod. "Okay. I got you, girl," she said.

"Thanks," Lissa said and turned back to her computer screen.

"Here ya go," Vickie said, putting a cup of coffee in front of her. She lowered her voice. "Good luck with that whole privacy thing."

Hours later, Lissa left the office and walked toward the rooming house.

An SUV slowed beside her. The window lowered. "Hey," Gage said. "Want a ride?"

"Am I going away from the inquisitions?" she asked.

"No questions from me," he said and she heard the sound of the doors unlocking.

Lissa opened the door and stepped inside the SUV. "This has been an interesting day."

"Part of your decision to get involved with the local sheriff. Are you sure you want to continue?" he asked.

She reached up to kiss him and chuckled. "How can I resist the most fabulous man I've ever met?"

Chapter Six

They spent the night making love. The next morning, Lissa had to be up early so she could greet her next group of volunteers at the church. Her cell phone alarm went off and she had to drag herself out of a sexual coma. "Oh, please help me," she murmured.

"I'm here for you, darlin'," Gage said, wrapping his arms around her.

"Stop it," she said, snuggling against him.

He chuckled and she loved that sound. It rippled inside her all the way to her heart. "You really want me to stop?" he asked.

She sighed. "Not really. I just need to get going so I can do my job. So I can help Rust Creek."

"Can't argue with that," Gage said. "Although I'd like to keep you here with me all day and all night. I guess I have to kick your gorgeous butt out of bed."

She smiled. "I guess you do."

Lissa and Gage took another joint shower and he got ready before she did. Darn him. This time, at least, she had fresh clothes. She'd decided to pack a set after that first night. While she was getting dressed, he was doing some chores with the horses.

When Gage came back, he fixed some kind of frozen egg biscuit. It wasn't nearly up to par with what Melba would have served, but after their busy night together, Lissa was grateful for anything. She made a mental note to fix breakfast next time.

He helped her into his SUV and they drove into town.

"You go into the office first," he said. "I don't want you taking heat because we're coming in at the same time. It could hurt your reputation."

She did a double take. "My reputation?" she echoed. "I would think it would improve my reputation if people knew you and I were involved."

He gave a slow grin. "Okay, you flatter me. I'm trying to protect you," he said.

"What are they going to say about me? That I've fallen under the sheriff's spell and want to spend every spare minute with him?" she asked.

He groaned. "You're just making it worse. I don't want them to think you're—"

"What? A wild, loose woman?" she asked.

"Well, I don't want anyone calling you—" He broke off. "I don't want to have to punch anyone."

Lissa laughed. "If someone's going to call me a loose woman because I'm involved with you, I'm okay with it. I'll just tell them we're lucky we're together."

He took a deep breath. "You're something else, Lissa," he said. "But go ahead into the office. I'll park the car and come in soon."

"Okay," she said and clutched his coat and pulled him closer. Then she kissed him and she didn't care who was looking.

She pulled back. "There I go, being a tramp. Heaven help me," she said and got out of the car.

"Heaven help *me,*" Gage said just before she closed the door behind her.

Lissa walked out into the cold fresh air and took a long breath. She could face anything if she had Gage. Scary thought that he had such a huge effect on her, but she wasn't going to question it. She was just going to go with it.

She walked into the office to find Vickie on the phone. Lissa waved and smiled then went to get some coffee. A few minutes later, Gage strode into the office. He also waved to Vickie and gave a nod to Lissa.

Lissa worked on her planned itinerary for the day, but she was distracted when still another visitor came through the door. *Grand Central Station?* she wondered.

"Hi, I'm Danielle Hawthorn here with my son Buddy," the woman said. "School's out today and I was hoping Buddy could volunteer with someone."

Gage came out of his office and glanced at the woman. "Danielle," he said.

"Yeah, you mentioned Buddy might be able to volunteer...."

"He can come with us," Lissa said impulsively. "I'm sure we'll have room. If that's okay with you."

"What are you doing?" Danielle asked.

"Flood relief," Lissa said.

"Perfect." She turned to her son. "I'll pick you up at the end of the day. In the meantime, be a good man."

Gage nodded. "We'll see you then," he said, then turned to the gangly teen who looked a bit awkward. "We're glad to have you. Buddy. This is Miss Roarke. She's been helping us repair some of the damage caused by the flood. Do you know anyone who got hit by the flood?"

Buddy nodded. "Lots of my friends. Some of them had to move into trailers."

"Miss Roarke has a crew of volunteers that will be out working today. You just do whatever she tells you," Gage said.

Buddy gave another nod. "Yes, sir."

Lissa extended her hand to the teen. "Buddy, it's nice to meet you and I'm so happy you'll be helping us today. We're leaving in a few minutes from the church parking lot, so we need to get over there right away." She turned to Gage. "Headed out."

"If you need me for anything…"

Lissa smiled. "I'll call you," she said and led Buddy out the door.

At the first house, the team did quite a bit of hammering to replace wooden construction damaged by the flood. A drywall team would finish the job the following day and with any luck, the displaced family would be able to return to their home this week. The crew ate sandwiches in the van. There was enough for Buddy to eat two. In the second house, owned by the Claibornes, the young family had tried to make do despite the damage. Buddy jumped right in to help, removing curtains and upholstered furniture.

Lissa updated the list of replacement items the home would need with the young mother while the children stayed with a neighbor.

"New sofa and at least one upholstered chair. New curtains. How are the curtains in the rest of the house?" she asked the woman.

"I think the ones upstairs are fine. I'm more concerned about the kitchen floor," Mrs. Claiborne said.

"We can take care of that, but it may not be until next week. How are your appliances?"

"My husband, John, saved those by putting them up on some blocks."

"Good for you," Lissa said.

Buddy stepped toward her, holding a musty, moldy, stuffed long-eared bunny. "Miss Roarke, I found this under the sofa," he said, lifting the animal toward her. "What should I do with it?"

"Oh, no," the young mother said. "That's Sara's bunny. We thought the flood washed it away. She's missed it so much. I wish there was some way to save it. I can't tell you how many times she has cried for that bunny."

Buddy looked at the bunny. "Could we wash it?"

"I think it's past saving, unfortunately. Maybe we should add a long-eared bunny to the list?" Lissa asked.

Buddy nodded. "My sister has a little stuffed dog and she screams whenever she can't find it."

Lissa gave him a commiserating smile and squeezed his shoulder. "Sounds like you have a lot of experience with this kind of thing. Thank you for bringing it to my attention."

An hour later, Lissa drove the van back to town. She thanked the crew members for their hard work and promised more tomorrow. They laughed in return. She was glad the townspeople had been so generous about helping with meals. She could rest easy knowing the volunteers would be well fed with a potluck dinner at the church tonight.

"I bet you're tired," she said to Buddy. "We can head back to the sheriff's office. Your mother should be there soon."

"Miss Roarke, would it be okay if we go to Crawford's General Store first? There's something I want to look at," Buddy said.

His request took her by surprise, but she couldn't see anything wrong with it, especially if she went with him. "Of course. I haven't been in the store very much myself except to buy yogurt, so I wouldn't mind a chance to look around in there a little bit."

Walking toward the store, Lissa made conversation with Buddy, asking him about his favorite classes and favorite things to do.

"I like math, but I hate English. I hate writing papers. It's so boring," he said.

"It's good that you like math. Trust me, you'll use it your whole life. But you need to do well in English, too. You'll be writing your whole life, too, one way or another. Even if you're just texting or sending emails. When you grow up and get a job you can't use all those abbreviations like LOL with your coworkers."

"Yeah, that's what my mother says," he said in a glum voice.

Lissa chuckled and opened the door of the General Store. "I'll meet you up front in about five minutes. Okay?"

Buddy nodded and headed toward the back of the store as if he were looking for something specific. Lissa felt as if she were taking a step back in time as she perused the store. Bags of feed and hardware lined shelves and bins, and groceries took the next aisle. Personal care items were arranged on an end cap. Beer and a very few varieties of wine sat in the refrigerated cases. She thought about grabbing a couple cartons of yogurt even though Melba fed her enough breakfast for three people. Recalling the greasy mystery biscuit Gage had offered her this morning, she decided to buy a few cartons along with some fruit.

As she approached the checkout, she saw that Buddy was holding a bag. "What did you buy?" she asked after the clerk rang her purchase.

"A bunny," he said proudly, pulling the stuffed animal from the bag. "It was marked down and I still didn't have enough money, but Mr. Morris said he would cover it for me when I told him why I was buying it."

Lissa's heart swelled with emotion. "Well, if that isn't the nicest thing… I think you should be the one to give the bunny to that little girl."

Buddy shrugged. "I don't know if I can. I've got to go to school tomorrow," he said.

"Maybe we can find someone to give you a ride out there," she said.

"I don't know. I know my mom can't do it. She's working two jobs," he said.

"We'll see," she said as she pushed open the door and walked down the street to the sheriff's office.

She and Buddy walked inside. His mother and Gage looked up as they entered.

"There you are," Danielle said. "I was getting a little worried."

Gage lifted his eyebrows in silent inquiry.

"We did a little shopping. Buddy purchased a stuffed bunny for a little girl whose toy was destroyed in the flood. How's that for being a good man?" she asked.

Danielle dropped her jaw and her eyes grew shiny with tears. "I don't know what to say." She stepped forward and drew her son into her arms. "I'm so proud of you."

"Aw, Mom," he said with a combination of embarrassment and pleasure.

Lissa felt herself tearing up at the sight of the mother and the teen boy. "I think it would be great if he could deliver the bunny personally. Maybe we can work out a time," she said hopefully.

Danielle pulled back and gave a big nod. "We can do that. I'd like to bring Buddy's brother and sister along, too, if you don't mind."

"Mom," Buddy protested.

"This will be a good example for both of them," Danielle insisted. She looked from Gage to Lissa. "I can't thank you enough."

"I need to thank *you*," Lissa said. "Buddy was a hard worker today."

"I can help again sometime if you need me," he said.

"You just said the magic words," Gage said. "I'm sure Miss Roarke will be calling on you." He patted the teen on his shoulder. "Good job today."

"Thanks," Buddy muttered.

Lissa watched them leave with a smile on her face.

Gage led her back to his office. "And for your next miracle, what are you going to do?"

"I didn't do anything," she said. "He really worked hard."

"I'm sure your enthusiasm and praise had nothing to do with it," he said.

She hesitated. "Not that much. He just already had a good heart."

"One step away from detention or forced community service," he said.

"Oh, you're exaggerating," she said. "He's a good kid. You know it. Everyone gets into a little trouble sometime," she said.

"When did you?" he asked.

Lissa gave a sheepish smile. "Well, there was

this one time I landed a borrowed car in a snowy ditch."

"Sounds like an accident," he said.

"And another time there was this little incident in a bar," she said.

"That resulted in multiple arrests," he said sourly. "What about your misspent youth?"

"I skipped school once," she said. "Got caught. I always get caught."

"Get caught doing what?" he returned, sliding his hand down to take hers.

"Got caught drinking a beer in my neighbor's backyard. We lived in a suburb just outside the city. I really couldn't get away with anything," she said, liking the way his fingers felt laced around hers.

"It's a wonder you didn't go wild when you had the chance," he said.

"By then, I didn't want to disappoint them. I wanted them to believe in me." She thought about how her parents had always seemed more proud of her brothers. One was a lawyer, the other worked for a big financial institution. "I guess I still want them to believe in me."

"Don't they?" he asked.

"I don't know. I'm not sure they're all that impressed with my career. I've done some writing along the way and they've always told me not to count on that to make a living."

"You should let me read some of your writing. I bet you're good," he said.

"How would you know that if you haven't read anything I've written?" she asked.

"Because I've watched you. And you're very good at everything you put your energy toward," he said in a sexy voice just before he kissed her. "Shh," he said and kissed her again.

Lissa sighed at the sensation of his lips on hers. It was all she could do not to fling herself at him. Pulling back, she sighed again. "I have some work I have to do tonight."

"Well, damn. I was hoping you would work on me," he said with a wicked grin.

She playfully punched his chest.

"You can stay and have dinner here, can't you?" he suggested.

"Dinner?" she echoed with surprise. "What are we going to eat? Breakfast muffins?"

Gage shook his head. "No. Mrs. Little brought in some lasagna. She said she baked enough for the potluck and had some left over."

"Oh, lasagna," Lissa said, her mouth watering. "I can't remember the last time I ate lasagna."

"I'll take that as a yes. Can't offer you any wine in the sheriff's office, though," he said.

"No problem," she said. "The sheriff already makes me feel a little dizzy."

"Is that so?" he said more than asked and pulled her against him again for another kiss.

Lissa and Gage ate their dinner in his office. He cleared off a corner of his desk and talked about the day. She was amazed by the variety of his tasks throughout the day, let alone each week. She glanced at her watch and saw that an hour had passed. She wondered how it had gone by so quickly.

She helped clear up from the meal. "As much as I would love to stay longer, I've got to coordinate some plans for later in the week."

"I understand," he said and pulled on his coat. "I'll walk you to the rooming house."

"But…" she began then broke off, hesitating to say what was on her mind.

"But what?" he asked, helping her put on her jacket.

"I thought you wanted to keep our relationship on the down low. If people see me spending time with you, then they're going to talk."

"We're okay as long as we don't flaunt it. It's not like I'll be taking you to the bar and dancing with you every night," he said.

"It would be nice to dance with you sometime," she said wistfully.

"I'm not much of a dancer," he said.

"We'll see," she said as he opened the door for her. They walked slowly down the street, chatting about anything and everything. When they arrived at the rooming house, she looked up at him. "Better not kiss me," she teased. "We're on the down low."

He shook his head. "You're just determined to cause trouble, aren't you?"

"Who? Me?" she asked, deliberately widening her eyes in mock innocence.

He tugged her toward a huge tree away from the bright porch light from the house and took her mouth in a passionate kiss. Her heart and breath did crazy things in response. When he finally pulled back, she could hardly breathe.

"I think you're the one causing trouble," she said. "And I like it very much."

"Hush," he said, putting his finger to her lips. "We'll just have to finish this trouble some other time. 'Night."

"Good night," she said and wobbled up the porch steps.

Gage decided to stop by the bar before he headed home. He would have much preferred spending his evening with Lissa, but he understood her need to work. She was making things happen in a way he'd never expected. He shouldn't have underestimated her.

He spotted his longtime friend Dallas Traub at

the bar and grabbed the stool next to him. "How's it going?" he asked him.

"As well as it can be. You want a beer?" Dallas asked.

Gage nodded and lifted his finger to the bartender.

"The election for mayor looks like it could get a little interesting," Dallas said.

"Yes. It was so much easier when we had Hunter McGee. I don't know anyone who didn't like him," Gage said, feeling the familiar stab of grief over the former mayor's death.

"Well, it gives people something to talk about," Dallas said and shot him a sideways glance. "Along with that pretty thing from New York who is providing flood relief."

"Yeah. Lissa Roarke is doing a good job. Surprises me how much she's getting done. She has a new set of volunteers rolling in every few days," Gage said.

"I also hear she's spending her extra time with the local sheriff," Dallas said.

Gage rolled his eyes. "Come on, Dallas. You know I don't talk about that kind of thing."

"You may not, but everyone else is," Dallas said and took a gulp from his beer.

"It's nobody's business," Gage said. "We've been keeping things discreet. I don't want people talking about her."

"Too late for that. Sounds like you may have already fallen for her," Dallas said. "Don't get ahead of yourself. Make sure you really get to know her before you get too involved. I sure as hell wish I'd done things differently with my ex-wife. Married her way too fast and it's going to take years to undo the damage."

Gage knew Dallas was recently divorced from his wife and pretty bitter about women in general. "Not every woman is like your ex-wife," Gage said.

"Maybe not," Dallas said. "But you take your time. Don't jump into the frying pan."

Frustration tugged at Gage. "What is this? Trust me, I haven't had any discussions about the future with Lissa," he said. "We both know she's leaving Rust Creek."

"Good. You just keep that in mind. But speaking of women, I heard you had dinner with Jasmine Cates," Dallas said. "How'd that go?"

Gage rolled his eyes. Sometimes he couldn't believe how much people talked about nothing in Rust Creek. He shrugged and took another sip of beer. "She ate a meal at the office with me. Nothing there."

"Hmm," Dallas said. "I spent some time with her, too."

"Really?" Gage said. "I'm glad to hear you're getting out."

Dallas scowled at him.

"Hey, if the shoe fits," Gage said, then changed the subject. "What do you think about those Broncos?"

"It's gonna take more than a star quarterback to pull everything together," Dallas said. "I'd like to see Seattle shake things up."

Gage nodded and took another sip of beer. He'd walked into the bar in a good mood, but talking with Dallas had ruined it for him.

The next morning, just before he left the trailer to do some morning chores, he received a call from his mother. "We haven't seen you in two weeks. Come over for dinner," she said.

Gage raked his hand through his hair. "Aw, Mom, you know how busy I've been. I don't know if I can make dinner tonight, but I'll try to stop by in the next day or two."

His mother gave a big sigh. "I realize you touch base with your father several times a week about ranch business, but I would like to hear from you, too," she said.

Gage felt the guilt screws sinking into his flesh. "I'm sorry, but you know that when I agreed to run for sheriff, my extra time was going to fly out the window. Add in the flood and it's been tough. I'll feel better about things when we see some light at the end of the tunnel. I just wish we could find the funds to get the school rebuilt."

"I know," she said. "But that's a lot of money and a lot of people are hurting these days. Speaking of the flood, though, I hear that volunteer coordinator from New York is very pretty."

Gage felt a twist of dread. He knew where this was headed. "Uh-huh. How's my sister doing?" he asked, trying to derail whatever comments his mother might make about his love life.

"She's fine. In love. But back to that volunteer coordinator. One of my friends told me that you've been seeing her," she said.

"Of course I see her," he said. "Her headquarters is pretty much run from the sheriff's office."

"That's not what I'm saying and you know it," his mother said. "Why is it that I have to hear from a friend that you've started seeing a woman?"

"Probably because you have a life and you're not nearly as gossipy as most of the women in town," Gage said.

"Well, thank you for that," she said. "But I wouldn't be a good mother if I didn't tell you to be careful. You're a good man and most of the single women in Rust Creek would love to be the object of your affection. You should focus on the local girls. This girl is from the city and you know how city people can be. They get bored."

Gage swallowed a sigh. "Thanks, Mom. Glad to know you think I'm boring."

"I didn't say that," his mother said. "I'm just feeling protective."

Gage's heart softened. "That's nice of you, Mom. But you and Dad raised me well and I'm all grown up now. I can take care of myself."

At that, his mother backed down. After a few more moments of small talk, he hung up the phone and groaned. *Why* did people feel the need to give him advice when he hadn't asked for it? He could only hope that no one else would offer commentary on his relationship with Lissa.

Chapter Seven

Lissa worked with her crew of volunteers nearly nonstop for the next three days. Gage barely got to see her for more than fifteen minutes at a time, and although he would pull out his teeth before he'd admit it, he was feeling cranky. Of course, his not seeing Lissa didn't keep people from making comments.

Vickie, the dispatcher, told him to go for it because he "deserved some good lovin'." He got another go-ahead from someone he stopped for speeding. And his deputy, Will, had clearly heard the rumors about Gage and Lissa. Clearly miffed, Will was only speaking to Gage when absolutely necessary.

All this waiting motivated Gage to do a little planning for the next time they got together. He bought wine from the general store—all three kinds. He bought some beer and steaks, along with potatoes, a large can of green beans and some biscuits. Most of what he bought was frozen or canned, so the fresh steaks and potatoes were a stretch for him.

The volunteer crew finally finished a half day of work and left to return home. Lissa walked into the office carrying a bag of something that smelled really good from the deli. "I'm finally done for two days. Barbecue sandwiches for everyone," she said.

"I'm not turning that down," Will said, bounding from his desk.

"Me, either," Vickie said. "Oh, look, you got eight sandwiches. Can I take an extra one home for dinner?"

"Feel free," Lissa said and met Gage's gaze. "Whew. What a crazy busy few days."

"I'll say," he said and accepted one of the sandwiches. "Come on in my office."

"Let me grab a drink first," she said and filled a cup from the water cooler.

She walked into his office and collapsed in the chair across from his desk. Her hair was tousled and her eyes had slight shadows beneath them. "You don't have to kill yourself for this."

"I'm not. I just want to maximize the volunteers when I have them. When they arrive, they want to work longer than I planned for them." She shrugged. "I'm just glad we've had a great combination of skilled and enthusiastic volunteers."

Gage nodded as she took a few bites. "What do you have planned for tonight?" he asked.

She pushed back her hair and smiled. "Besides sleeping?"

"Any chance you'd like to sleep at my place?" he asked.

Her eyes brightened. "How much will I get to sleep at your place?" she asked, leaning forward.

Something about her made him want to eat her up. "I'll let you sleep just as much as you want," he said, and bit into his sandwich.

She gave a low, sexy chuckle. "The trouble is I don't want to sleep when I'm with you. What are you going to feed me for dinner?" she asked.

"Steak and baked potato," he said, feeling a bit proud that he'd already planned the menu.

She widened her eyes. "Really? I didn't know you had anything like that in your kitchen."

"I didn't until last night," he said.

She laughed and the sound made everything inside him feel a little lighter. "Then you've got yourself a date, Sheriff. I'll wrap up some paperwork."

"And take a nap," he told her. They traded bites of their sandwiches with conversation.

"Is that an order?" she asked, tilting her head at a challenging angle.

"A word of encouragement," he said.

"Sort of like the same words you offer people who may end up in jail if they don't follow your encouragement?" she asked.

"You're in no danger of ending up in jail," he promised. "I've just been missing you," he said, surprising himself with the admission.

She blinked then took a slow breath. "I've been missing you, too. I'll try to squeeze in a nap, Sheriff."

"Thanks for the sandwiches," he said and crumpled his wrapper.

She stood and shrugged. "My way of celebrating."

It was all he could do not to pull her into his arms, but Gage knew once he touched her, he wouldn't want to stop. "Later," he said.

"Yeah, later," she said in a husky voice and left his office.

Lissa did as much work as possible then forced herself to lie down for a short time. She was so looking forward to her evening with Gage that she had a hard time settling down. As soon as she fell asleep, however, she heard her cell phone beep.

Lissa dragged her head off the pillow and answered. "Hi," she said.

"You sound dead to the world," Gage said.

She was half awake. His voice made her stomach flip-flop. It was an involuntary response. "I'm awake," she said, propping herself up against her pillow. She took a deep breath and almost slapped herself so she would sound more perky.

"Yeah," he said. "I just wouldn't want you performing surgery or driving a car," he said.

She frowned into the phone. "I don't have to do either, do I?" she asked.

"Good point," he said. "Are you ready? I'm waiting out front of the rooming house," he said.

Yikes. "Sure," she lied. "Give me two minutes. Maybe three," she said as she rose from the bed.

He chuckled. "I'll give you five. Don't trip down the stairs."

"Okay, okay. See you soon," she said and turned off the phone. Racing toward the bathroom, she splashed her face and brushed her teeth. She grabbed her toothbrush, deodorant and moisturizer, then added some clean clothes and cartons of yogurt and an apple from her minifridge to the pile and threw everything into a tote bag and headed out the door. Lissa was one of the few guests with a minifridge in her room. Apparently, the previous guest in her room had needed to refrigerate their medication for a chronic medical condition.

She skidded to a halt at the top of the steps, remembering Gage's words. *Don't trip.* Swearing under her breath, she carefully descended the stairs, running into Melba.

"Well, hi there, darling," Melba said. "Where are you headed?"

Lissa felt a sudden twist of inexplicable embarrassment and guilt. She felt as if her mother had caught her headed out the door for trouble. Where had that come from, she wondered. She was a grown woman. She shouldn't have to explain herself to anyone.

"I'm going out," she said. "A friend invited me to take a break tonight. I'll be back tomorrow."

Melba gave a slow nod. "That sounds like a good friend," the older woman said. "Just don't get into trouble."

"I won't," Lissa said, barely able to keep the laughter from her voice. She was headed straight for trouble. The best kind of trouble.

She scuttled out the front door and down the porch steps to Gage's SUV parked discreetly several yards from the front of the house. She raced into the vehicle and tossed her tote into the backseat. "Whew, that was interesting," she said.

"Mama Melba grill you?" he asked.

She sighed. "It wasn't exactly grilling, but I felt like I was facing both my mom and dad when I was trying to get away with something."

"How'd that work out?" he asked.

"She told me not to get into trouble," she said.

Gage gave a dirty laugh and shifted the card into drive.

The car was nice and cozy and Gage had put low music on the radio. Lissa got so comfortable she drifted to sleep. Sometime later, the SUV hit a bump that awakened her. Lissa glanced at Gage. "How long have I been asleep?"

"Since three minutes after you got in the car," he said.

"Why didn't you wake me up?"

"I want you to get all the rest you can," he said and smiled at her. "I'd like you to stay awake at least for the steak I'm going to cook for you."

"I'm sorry," she said. "I feel like I have sleeping sickness."

"You've been running on adrenaline. You just need a little nap," he said as he pulled in front of his trailer.

"I'm sorry I've been boring," she said.

"You're not boring," he said. "You're pretty whether you're awake or asleep."

His words eased something inside her. "Thanks," she said.

"Just speaking the truth," he said.

He got out of the car and walked to her side of the car to help her out of the door. She was always surprised by his chivalry. Perhaps she'd lived in Manhattan too long, where the men pretty much shoved you out of the cab after a date if they didn't think you were going to put out.

The sky was a dark velvet blanket with bright stars "It's so beautiful tonight," she said, breathing in the crisp night air.

"Yeah, you are," he said.

She swatted at him. "Stop flattering me," she said.

"Come on inside," he said, leading her inside the trailer. He grabbed the potatoes, washed them and tossed them in the microwave. He put the green beans to warm on the stove and took the steaks out to put on his small gas grill.

"You're so efficient. I don't know what to say," she said.

"I forgot the biscuits. Can you put them in the oven?"

"Sure," she said and returned to the trailer to take care of the bread for dinner. Being with Gage made her feel more energized. After the crew left, Lissa had felt as if she could go into a coma, but Gage brought her back to life. Setting a timer for the biscuits on her cell phone, she went outside to join Gage.

He flipped the steaks. "Biscuits okay?"

"Perfect," she said. "I'm very impressed by this meal. What inspired you?"

"You," he said without hesitation. "I got a little grumpy when I didn't get to spend time with you the past few days. I decided you deserved a good meal, and I was determined to give it to you."

His confession twisted her heart. "That's the nicest thing anyone has ever done for me."

He met her gaze. "You deserve more."

Her heart tripped over itself. "Sheriff, are you trying to get me into trouble?"

He smiled and pulled her against him, taking her mouth in a deep kiss. "I'm doing my best."

Several moments later, everything was ready and Lissa joined Gage for the hearty meal. "Delicious," she told him as she took a bite of steak.

"I aim to please," he said.

Afterward, they went outside and cuddled in the moonlight. "It's so quiet here," she said. "I can't remember being in such a quiet, beautiful place."

"That's our specialty in Montana," he said and looked upward. "That and our wide-open skies."

"It's calming and peaceful," she said.

"A lot different than Manhattan," he said.

"Yes." She took a deep breath. "I hear a song in my head. Perfect for a dance in the Montana moonlight. Would you join me?"

He paused a moment. "You'll have to hum it so I get the beat right," he said.

Seconds later, he pressed one hand against her back and lifted her hand with the other. She hummed under her breath, but he caught on. Soon enough, they were waltzing.

Lissa looked into his face and everything in side her jumped and screamed. She had been waiting for this moment her entire life. Gage was her dream come true.

"You lied," she said breathlessly.

Gage frowned, but didn't miss a step. "What do you mean?"

"You're a great dancer," she said. "The very best."

Gage lifted his head, his throat bared to her as he laughed. "It's the moonlight and the stars fooling you," he said. "They're on my side tonight."

After a night filled with lovemaking and some sleep, Lissa awakened the next morning when she felt Gage rise from the bed. "Hey, is it already time to get up?" she asked, already missing his body next to hers.

"It is for me, sleepyhead. But you can get a few more winks if you like," he said and smiled at her.

"What are you going to do?"

"I've got to ride my horses every now and then to keep them from getting green." Seeing her confused look, he clarified, "That means I would have to do a lot of re-training and conditioning with them. It won't take long," he said and brushed his hand over her hair.

"Can I go with you?"

"You ride?"

"Well, I have," she said. "It's been a while."

"Okay. We can take it slow on the ride, but you better hop out of bed."

She sat up and wiped the sleep from her eyes. "I can move quickly. Just let me splash some water on my face and brush my teeth."

"I can heat up a frozen breakfast biscuit for you," he offered.

"No need," she said, slipping past him to the tiny bathroom. "I brought my own fruit this time. I'll skip your mystery meat, thank you."

"Mystery meat?" he echoed. "What do you mean?"

"Have you read the ingredients on the package?" she asked as she splashed her face. "How many of them can you pronounce?"

"I didn't know you were a health nut," he said.

"I'm not. I just like to be able to pronounce what I'm putting in my body." She brushed her teeth.

"Picky, picky," he teased. "You think those muffins we get at the office are chemical free?"

She didn't argue. She was too busy getting dressed and pulling her hair into a low ponytail. Lissa was excited to go horseback riding. It had been ages since she'd ridden. Within moments, she and Gage tramped to the barn. He saddled up a sweet, aging mare named Sally for her and a gelding named Black for himself.

"I'll lead with Black. He can get a little cantankerous, and I don't want him irritating Sally. You won't have to do much with her. She knows the way and she's got a soft mouth. Let's move along," he said and made a clicking sound.

As they climbed a hill, Lissa marveled at the view. "It's so beautiful and clear. It really does seem like I can see for miles."

"That's what we're known for—wide-open spaces. There's a reason we're called big sky country. A lot different than what you see every day in Manhattan, that's for sure."

"What surprises me is how quiet it is out here. There's always some kind of noise in the city," she said.

"Yeah, people either love it or the isolation eventually drives them crazy. The winters can be pretty harsh here. Add in the lack of accessibility to entertainment and shopping and it's tough to face it on an everyday basis when you're used to having everything within walking distance."

Lissa nodded, wondering if she could see herself living full time in Montana. She honestly hadn't missed New York at all since she'd set foot here. "I haven't gone through a winter here, so I can't really make that call. But it's not like you've got to hitch a wagon to go to town. You can drive."

"As long as you can drive in the snow," he said in a meaningful voice.

She made a face at him. "You're never going to

let me live that down, are you? If I'm such a rotten winter driver, then maybe you should teach me."

"I'll do that," he said, meeting her gaze. "If you're here when it snows again."

His comment stabbed at her. Both of them knew her stay in Montana was only temporary, but she didn't want to think about her time with Gage coming to an end.

After they finished their ride, Gage checked out the rest of the horses and let them into the pasture. "Hmm," he said as he watched for a moment.

"What's the problem?"

"It looks like Damien might be favoring his right side," he said, pointing to a brown horse. "I'll have to check that out later. Let's head back to my place."

Walking back to Gage's trailer, they passed by his house. She paused. "You never showed me your house," she said.

"There's not much to see downstairs. I took out all the upholstered furniture. It's iffy whether I'll need a new floor. I lost the stove and fridge, too."

"Have you filed for any compensation?" she asked.

"Just haven't gotten around to it. The drywall will have to be replaced in one of the rooms. I've already torn out the bad stuff and I ran fans in there like crazy afterward. I'll get to it sometime. Maybe next spring. Why should I get back into my house when there are families still waiting to get back into theirs?"

"Well, why shouldn't you get back into your house?" she asked.

He shrugged. "My house is not a priority," he said. "You take the first shower. I'm going to take care of a few chores."

Staring after Gage, Lissa blinked. He'd sounded almost curt. She admired the sacrifices he was making for the other citizens in his area, but she didn't think he needed to be last in line for repairs. Gage worked his butt off for the community. He could use a little comfort during the few hours he was at home.

Chewing on some possibilities, she took her shower, toweled off and got dressed. When Gage returned, he also took a shower, letting out a shout after a few minutes.

Alarmed, Lissa tapped on the door, carrying her carton of yogurt with her. "What's wrong?"

"Ran out of hot water. It's damn cold," he said.

"Yikes," she said. "Sorry."

Gage stepped from the minuscule bathroom with a towel wrapped around his waist. "No problem. The trailer's stingy with hot water. I'm glad you got yours first."

"Now I feel bad," she said.

"I'll let you make it up to me," he said with a

grin and pressed a quick kiss on her mouth. "Are my lips blue?"

"No," she said with a laugh, admiring his well-muscled body. "You look like you survived the frigid temperature pretty well."

"Sure I did. We need to eat and hit the road. Is that yogurt any good?" he asked.

"Yummy peach," she said. "I've also got blueberry."

"I like blueberries. I'll give that one a try," he said.

Not that she had offered, Lissa thought, but smiled at the notion that she had influenced him even a tiny bit. He ate two cartons of yogurt and one of her apples.

Apparently Gage liked the food choices suggested for him.

They made it into town and Gage let her off at the rooming house. Lissa prayed she could make it up the back stairway without Melba confronting her. After making it to her room, she breathed a sigh a relief then sank onto the bed. More than anything, she wanted to take a nap. A long nap.

Torn, she dragged herself out of bed. She had fresh volunteers arriving in two days, and she needed to map out a schedule. No rest for the wicked or pure, she thought. And she sure as heck wasn't pure.

Lissa grabbed her iPad and sat in a straight-backed chair. She decided to skip going to headquarters and focus on working here in her room. Maybe later she could squeeze in a nap.

Just after two o'clock in the afternoon, she'd made dozens of lists and schedules and several appointments and her eyes were drooping, so she took that well-needed nap. She set her alarm for two hours.

Lissa was awakened by an annoying beeping sound. It took her several seconds, but she finally realized the sound was coming from her phone. Oh, wow, she could use some more sleep, she thought. Like maybe twenty-four hours.

That wasn't going to happen, she realized, and stumbled into her bathroom to splash water on her face and brush her teeth. It was her customized routine for waking up when she wanted sleep more than anything.

While she was brushing her teeth, her cell phone rang. She rinsed her mouth then picked up. "Hi," she said.

"Hi. Are you coming back to life?" Gage said.

"I'm doing the best I can," she said.

"Bet you're sore from your morning ride," he said.

She frowned. "Bet you're right. How did you know?"

"Riding uses different muscles. You want to take a break and stay at Melba's tonight?"

"No," she said. "But I do need some more sleep

because more volunteers are coming the day after tomorrow."

"You want me to keep my hands off you?" Gage asked.

"Never," she said.

He chuckled. "I'll pick you up in a few. Look for my car," he said.

"You might want to pick up a couple cartons of yogurt and some fruit," she said.

"Okay," he said. "By the way, I forgot to tell you, but I bought some wine a few days ago."

"You're a great guy," she said.

"Yeah, keep saying that," he said.

Lissa laughed. "You're a great guy. You're a great guy. You're a great—"

"Okay, stop or I'll get sick," he said.

"You're a great—"

Click. Lissa glanced at her phone and saw that Gage had disconnected the call. Even when she was half asleep, he made her feel alive. She grabbed a few items and a change of clothing. She glanced outside her window and saw Gage's SUV parked away from the light cascading over the front lawn.

Her heart skipped a beat and she gathered her belongings in a tote bag then made her way down the back stairway.

"Hey, sweetie," Melba said.

Dumb luck, Lissa thought. "Hi there, Melba," she said and gave the woman a big hug.

"You haven't shown up for breakfast lately," Melba said.

"I know. My schedule has been crazy. My volunteer group just left and a new one is coming in soon."

"Well, everyone is talking about everything you're getting done. You're a marvel. Let me know if there's anything I can do. I'll even let you use my car," the woman said.

"Oh, you're too sweet. Especially after I landed your car in the ditch."

"Bessie's been through more than a little trip in the ditch. And it's all for a good cause," she said. "Taking care of Rust Creek Falls. That's what we're trying to do."

"You're so right," Lissa said.

Melba sighed. "Well, I wish I could do more for you," she said.

"You've already done more than enough. You've given me a second home," Lissa said and hugged the woman again.

"You're a sweet girl," Melba said. "You call me anytime you need me."

Lissa's heart twisted as she headed out the back door and rushed toward Gage's vehicle. She climbed in and took a deep breath. "Hiya. Good to see you."

"Good to see *you*," he said.

"Thanks," she said and sank her head back against the seat.

"I need to let you sleep more tonight," he said.

"Oh, no," she protested. "Keep me awake," she said. "I love the way you keep me awake."

Gage groaned. "You send my good intentions to hell in a handbasket."

Chapter Eight

I'm so excited with the progress we're making in Rust Creek Falls. With new volunteer crews arriving every few days, we get a fresh group of people eager to work and make a difference. The people here are just as fantastic. They are providing meals for the volunteers and many of them are helping their neighbors with damaged homes even while their own homes have been damaged. Even the children are helping! The sheriff continues to work nearly 'round the clock to help everyone get back on their feet. He's an amazing man. I've never met anyone like

him and I'm growing more certain, day by
day, that I never will again. Sometimes I have
to pinch myself that I'm getting to know him
on such a deep level.

—*Lissa Roarke*

Gage savored another night with Lissa, but then the new set of volunteers arrived and she was busy all the time. It gave him an opportunity to stop by his parents' house for a few minutes and catch up on his chores. He checked out his horse, Damien, and decided to call his longtime friend Brooks Smith, the best veterinarian in the area, to come take a look. He'd known Brooks since the two had gone to high school together.

The animal doctor drove in from Livingston about two hours later.

Gage walked outside to meet Brooks. "Thanks for coming," he said, extending his hand. "I would have called your dad, but I hear he's not feeling well lately."

Brooks nodded. "He's not in the best health."

Gage led the way toward the barn. "When are you going to move back to town? It would make sense for you to take over your father's practice, especially if his health is failing."

Brooks frowned. "Try telling my father that. He's not ready to give the practice to me yet. He wants me to be married first," he said in disgust.

"Married?" Gage echoed. "What does being married have to do with taking over your dad's vet practice?"

"He thinks being married adds stability. It's not like I've gone tearing off to Alaska or anywhere else all the time."

Gage shrugged. "True. Maybe he'll come around," he said as they walked into the barn.

"I think he's determined that *I'm* the one who should come around." Brooks shook his head. "Having a wife is a time and energy drain. I don't have time for a wife, let alone a social life right now."

Gage thought about Lissa and how he'd been doing everything he could to avoid a social life until she came to town. "Sometimes a social life finds you even when you're not looking for it."

Brooks glanced at Gage. "Spoken like a man who has a woman on the brain."

Gage didn't like talking about his relationship with Lissa. People offered too many opinions. "I guess it depends on the woman. Some of them don't make it feel like a drain, but I'm no expert, that's for sure."

"I don't know any man who is an expert on women," Brooks said with a laugh. "Now let me take a look at your horse."

Brooks examined Damien and confirmed a mild tendon injury. "Ice and rest. Keep him in the stall.

You can put a gel cast on him then walk him in a few days. I don't recommend an anti-inflammatory in this case because he's more likely to rest the leg if it hurts. Call me if you run into any problems."

"Thanks for coming out," Gage said.

"Anytime," Brooks said as they returned to his truck.

"Good luck with your dad," Gage said.

Brooks gave a rough chuckle. "I'll need it. Take care, now."

Late that afternoon, Gage went into the office and was greeted by Lissa. She was so excited about something that she couldn't keep still. "What happened?" he asked. "Did you win the lottery?"

"In a way," she said. "Someone at Bootstraps has located a furniture store that's going out of business and they've agreed to donate a bunch of furniture to the flood victims in Rust Creek. One of the volunteers from my last crew called and they've raised money to donate new stuffed animals, linens and curtains."

"You're a regular miracle worker," he said, wanting to pick her up and hug her.

"Me?" she said. "It's not me. These are other people making these donations."

"Because you've gotten them all fired up," he said. "That's why your crews are getting twice as much done as you expected and why you're so perfect at what you do."

She stared at him for a half moment. "No one has ever accused me of being perfect," she said.

"Well, you're pretty darn close."

"Thank you," she said, "I could kiss you for that. The reason I'm here a little early tonight is because I'm meeting Buddy and his family out at the Claibornes' house. He's going to give the little girl her bunny. It's last minute, but his mother Danielle has a very hectic schedule. Would you like to go?"

"I'd be honored," he said. "Let me make a few calls and I'll tell Will he's in charge until I get back."

They left for the Claibornes' about thirty minutes later and pulled into the family's driveway with Buddy's family following right after. Gage and Lissa greeted Danielle and her children. Buddy carried a box wrapped in pink paper.

"Is that the bunny?" Lissa asked.

Buddy nodded. "My mom thought the little girl might like it even better if she got to unwrap it."

The small group made their way to the front door and were welcomed inside by Mrs. Claiborne. "Please, come in. Sara, say hello," she said, taking the hand of a young toddler with brown tousled curls looking up with wide blue eyes.

"Hi," Sara whispered then stuck her thumb in her mouth.

"She's a little shy," Mrs. Claiborne said. "Sara,

this young man has brought you a gift. Do you want to open it?"

Sara hesitated then nodded.

Buddy stepped forward and gave the little girl the wrapped gift. "I heard you were missing one of these and saw this. I hope you like it."

Sara plopped down on the floor and tore off the paper. Buddy helped her open the box.

She pulled the bunny from the box and gasped. "Bunny! It's Bunny," she said and hugged the stuffed animal against her.

Lissa's heart squeezed tight and she felt her eyes fill with tears. What Buddy had done was such a small, but powerful example of the generosity she'd seen in all the people of Rust Creek Falls. They'd sacrifice for themselves to make up for someone else's loss.

She felt Gage's arm around her and was so thankful for his strength.

"Buddy, I don't know how to thank you," Mrs. Claiborne said. "You've just made my Sara very happy."

Buddy shoved his hands in his pockets. "It was nothing," he said.

"No, it was something very nice," Mrs. Claiborne insisted. "Sara, tell Buddy thank you."

The little toddler rushed toward him and gave him a hug. "Thank you," she said.

Buddy's face turned red with embarrassment, but anyone could see he was pleased.

"I'm proud of you," Gage said. "You're growing up to be a good man."

"Thank you, Sheriff," he said.

"Well, I guess we should go now," said Buddy's mother, Danielle. "It was nice meeting you. I hope your little Sara will enjoy the bunny."

They said their goodbyes and returned to the driveway.

Danielle stopped and turned to Lissa and Gage. "I can't thank you enough," she said, lifting her hand to her throat. "I was starting to worry, but I can see Buddy's got a solid gold heart. With your help, I'll keep him moving in the right direction."

"Call if you need anything," Gage said. "We've got people volunteering to help with transportation."

"Let me know the next time he's off from school. I'd love for him to keep helping out," Lissa said.

"I'll do that," Danielle said and loaded her family into her car.

Gage opened the passenger door for Lissa and she stepped inside. As soon as she got inside, she burst into tears.

Gage shot her a worried look. "What's wrong?" he asked, taking her hand.

"It just got to me. You can tell Danielle is struggling to keep it all together and they don't have much money. Buddy has to feel the strain. He has a little money in his pocket and what does he do with it? Buys a bunny for some little girl he doesn't even know." She sniffled. "Sorry. It's just one of the sweetest things I've witnessed in a while."

He pulled her into his arms and she allowed herself to sink against him. "Like I said before, you're inspiring everyone to give more than usual."

"I can't take credit for this," she said and took a deep breath. "It's going to be hard for me to leave these people behind. I don't know how I'm going to do it," she said. "I didn't expect to get so attached."

Gage sucked in a quick breath, his eyes giving a stormy glint. "You'll be okay. You'll work it all out, get some perspective and move on."

How could he be so positive about her leaving? she wondered.

"Besides," he said, tipping up her chin with his finger. "You're not gone yet. You're still here. By the time you have to leave, all of us might succeed in driving you crazy." He dropped a kiss on her lips. "Don't think about leaving until it's time to go."

She sank her head against his chest. "If you say so," she said.

"I do."

One day later, Lissa's crew left and she had two days to prepare for the next group. The incoming volunteers had recently increased their numbers, so Lissa was reworking the schedule to accommodate the added volunteers. It was an unusually warm day and she sat in a chair in Gage's front yard. She could feel the heat of the sun on her face.

She sighed with pleasure. These little breaks in between the departures and arrivals of volunteer crews provided her with so many sweet moments with Gage. Every day she spent with him made her want more time with him.

Just up the hill, she could see him walking Damien, helping the horse in his healing process. That was who Gage was—a man determined to help those hurting and in need. Before she'd met him, Lissa would have thought of a sheriff as a tough guy, and Gage was certainly strong. But he was so much more than that. His sense of humor put people at ease even in the worst situations. He cared deeply for the people in Rust Creek Falls and they counted on him in return.

Distracted by her thoughts about Gage, she opened a file on her iPad and began to write about him, what he meant to the people of Rust Creek Falls and what he meant to her. She easily filled the next hour composing her thoughts about him until a shadow fell over her.

"Boo," Gage said and she nearly jumped out of the chair.

She put her hand to her racing heart. "You scared me."

"It was easy. You looked pretty intense. How's the scheduling coming?"

"Pretty good," she said. "I'm not quite done yet."

He picked her up, taking her by surprise, then plopped down on the chair with her in his lap. "You're awfully pretty sitting here in the sun, Miss Lissa."

She snuggled against him. "You're awfully pretty, too," she teased.

He chuckled. "You know a man doesn't like to be described as pretty."

"I think you're tough enough to handle it," she said.

He took her mouth in a kiss that made everything inside her melt. He pulled back just a bit, his eyes dark with arousal. "You look tired. I think you need to go back to bed."

"So, it's nap time?" she asked.

He rose and headed for the trailer. "Maybe later," he said.

They spent the next hour making sweet love. Lissa couldn't believe the combination of feelings he aroused in her. He made her so hungry for him, so crazy with wanting. She couldn't remember feeling safer and…more adored. Yes, adored.

At rest next to him after they'd pushed each

other to the limits then over the edge, her hand on his chest, she felt his heart pounding. The strong, sure beat called to her. She looked at his face and an earthshaking knowledge rocked through her. She was in love with Gage.

"You're staring," he said, his eyes still closed.

"You can't possibly know that," she said. "Your eyes are closed."

"I'm a lawman," he said. "I have eyes in the back of my head and I can see things even when I'm asleep."

"Hmm," she said. "Sounds like Santa Claus."

He let out a chuckle and pulled her on top of him. "You are one sassy woman, Lissa Roarke. A man would have a hard time keeping your mouth shut."

"You didn't want it shut a few moments ago," she told him breathlessly.

"Oh, don't remind me, or I'll have to take you again," he said as if the thought pained him.

"Would that be so bad?"

"No, but I need some sustenance if you're gonna keep wearing me out like this. Come on and fix me a sandwich," he said.

She loved the way he conveniently forgot that he had initiated their lovemaking, but she was too happy to dispute it. Pulling on her clothes, she headed for the tiny kitchen.

"I tell you it's hard to get any work done with

you around," he said after he'd pulled on his jeans and a shirt.

Work. The word juggled something in her mind and she panicked. "Oh, no. I left my iPad outside."

"Don't worry. I'm sure it's still there. I'll get it for you," he said and went outside.

Lissa was surprised to see that Gage had fresh bread and deli meat and cheese for sandwiches, but he'd told her he figured if he planned to keep her barricaded on his ranch, then he'd better be prepared to feed her. And him. It warmed her heart that he'd planned for their time together. She'd just finished preparing three sandwiches when her cell phone rang.

"Lissa Roarke," she said and pointed to the sandwiches as Gage returned with her tablet.

He nodded and sat down at the table, inhaling his food as he glanced at her iPad.

"Miss Roarke, this is Virginia Conner," the woman on the other end of the line said. "We're just going to need more beds. Five more people volunteered this morning."

"Well, that's fantastic," Lissa said. "I've got another day to figure this out. I'll call you tomorrow. Okay?"

Excited, she disconnected the call. "I need to call the minister and a few other women who've been helping with food. We are getting so many volunteers there won't be enough cots at the church for them. Isn't this fantastic?"

He smiled at her. "Sure is. That second sandwich is for me, right?" he asked.

Lissa laughed. "Of course it is."

While Lissa made her calls, Gage pushed the screen, thinking he'd play a game to kill some time. Instead of pulling up a game, however, the screen revealed a word document. Curious if this was some of the writing she'd mentioned to him, he scanned the first few sentences.

It didn't take long, however, for him to see that she was writing about him. Uncomfortable, he almost set the device aside, but he couldn't resist this opportunity to see inside her head. She described him as "her beautiful cowboy." Reading the words got under his skin. He shifted in his chair and continued to read. *He is the perfect man, the man I always dreamed I would find. I had begun to think such a man didn't exist until I met Gage.*

Gage raked his fingers through his hair. "Perfect," he muttered. "Nobody's perfect." He sure as hell wasn't. *He is strong, yet gentle and kind, the most honorable man I've ever known.*

Gage shook his head. He couldn't see himself in her description of him. She was writing about a man with a sterling character who had no flaws. Who'd never done anything wrong. The man Lissa wrote about had never failed anyone, and Gage knew he had failed a lot of people when he hadn't been here to help them during the flood.

His gut twisted and he pushed the tablet away from him along with the second sandwich. Lissa was a talented storyteller, no doubt, but she'd fallen for a man who didn't exist.

At that moment, Lissa bounded into the room. "We're covered," she said. "Three people have agreed to allow some of the volunteers to stay in their homes. The people here just keep outdoing themselves."

"Good," Gage said and stood. "Good job. Listen, I've got some more chores to do. I'll be back in a couple hours. Okay?"

"Okay. I'll be here when you get back. I may even take a nap," she said with a wink. She was clearly still so happy that nothing could bother her. Good, he thought, because he had no idea how to handle what he'd just read. No idea at all.

Lissa spent the night with Gage, relishing being so close to him. He made love to her again, but he didn't talk much afterward. She told herself she had just worn out her amazing cowboy. The next day, he let her off at Melba's with a quick kiss.

"We'll talk later," he said. He seemed a little distracted, but he also appeared to be in a hurry to get to the office, so she didn't question him.

Gage had a lot of people counting on him. She felt greedy about their time together because her assignment wasn't going to last forever. She'd decided yesterday, however, to ask her boss to grant her an extension. There was so much more she wanted to do.

The following day, the new crew arrived and since there were more people, there was more for her to do. She popped into the office to find Gage but he was gone. A perfect opportunity to put her plan into action, she seized the moment to chat with Vickie and Will.

"I'm going to ask a huge favor of you and I'm swearing you both to secrecy," she said after she'd persuaded Vickie to join her at Will's desk.

"Are you pregnant?" Vickie asked.

Lissa dropped her jaw and felt her cheeks heat with embarrassment. "Absolutely not."

"That's good to know," Will muttered. "What's this about? I've got work to do."

Lissa had noticed Will had become much less friendly to her since she and Gage had gotten involved. "I really do appreciate your cooperation. Sometime this week, I'm going to try to get the volunteers to fix Gage's house."

Vickie clapped her hands together in approval. "Perfect. He'd never do it on his own."

"You're right. He wouldn't," Will said. "Always puts himself last. What do you need from us?"

"I don't want him to make any unexpected trips home the day that we'll be doing the repairs."

"So, you want us to keep him busy?" Vickie asked.

"No," Lissa said. "I just want you to keep me informed if he decides to go home during the day we're doing repairs."

Vickie glanced at Will. "We should be able to do that. He doesn't sneak home very often, does he?"

Will rolled his eyes. "The sheriff doesn't *sneak* anywhere."

"Okay, then, are you in?"

"Of course," Vickie said.

"Yeah, I'm in," Will said a little more slowly. "He's a lucky guy."

Lissa spent the next several days dodging Gage. She feared he would be able to read her intentions without her saying a word. Avoiding him wasn't as difficult as she'd thought. A part of her was concerned, but she was so focused on renovations she couldn't get too upset.

Nut job, she called herself, but kept going. She didn't know how she and the volunteer group had pulled it off, but fifteen homes were repaired. The church held a banquet for the volunteers the night before they left and Lissa gave a speech, thanking everyone who had contributed. The volunteers would complete a few last-minute projects and leave late tomorrow afternoon.

After the volunteer banquet, Lissa walked toward the rooming house, feeling spent and tired. An SUV pulled alongside her as she walked, and the passenger window was lowered.

"Want a ride?" Gage asked.

"I'm just headed back to the rooming house," she said. "I'm almost there."

"I can give you a ride to my place," he said.

"I won't be much good for you tonight. I'm way past tired."

His gaze gentled. "No pressure," he said. "I'll let you sleep."

She took a deep breath, pulled open the door and climbed into the warm car. "I can't remember when I've been this tired."

"You've been a busy girl," he said.

"I don't have a change of clothes," she warned him.

"You can use one of my shirts," he said. "And I actually have a few extra cartons of yogurt in my fridge."

"Really?" she said, surprised. "I thought you preferred the mystery meat biscuit."

"I like that some days," he said defensively. "But that yogurt and fruit thing is nice, too."

"I can't believe I've had such influence over your eating habits," she said, leaning her head back against the headrest.

"Yeah, well, don't get too arrogant," he said.

"No chance of that," she said and closed her eyes.

Sometime later, she wasn't sure how long, she awakened to the sight of Gage hovering over her. She blinked. "Hi."

"You were snoring," he said.

"Sorry," she said. "I must have been very tired." She glanced around and saw that she was in the bed in his trailer. She leaned back her head, closed her eyes and sighed. "I don't know whether to ask for wine or ice cream."

"Ice cream?" he echoed.

"You don't have any?" she asked,

"I don't know. I might have some chocolate popsicles in the freezer," he said.

Lissa sat up in bed. "That sounds perfect."

He chuckled. "If you say so. Let me check."

He left the room and she closed her eyes again, wishing she weren't so tired. But oh, my goodness, what a week. And the irony was that Gage still didn't know that his home had been repaired. She laughed to herself that she and the workers had been able to pull it off. She couldn't wait to see his face when he realized what had been done. She hoped he would be pleased.

Chapter Nine

Lissa sat up and ate a chocolate sundae popsicle. "I don't want to know how many chemicals are in this," she said as she took a bite. "It's just too good."

"I bought these a few months ago," he said and took a bite of the same kind of popsicle.

"I like that it has several layers. Crunchy on top, then chocolate, then vanilla, then more chocolate." She took another bite. "Yum."

Gage looked at her eating the popsicle and felt unbearably aroused. He had hoped to avoid her, but he couldn't make himself. He wanted her in every possible way, sexually, mentally.... Every way.

"How can I think about eating ice cream when you're in my bed?" he asked.

She took another bite then offered the popsicle to him. "Will this help?" she asked.

He took a bite. "Not really."

She handed him the rest of the popsicle. "I'm ready to toss it and do something else," she said.

He took the popsicle away and returned. Lowering his mouth to hers, he began to remove her clothes. "I've missed you."

"I've missed you, too," she whispered and allowed him to sweep her away.

His sweet lovemaking took her to a different place where it was just Gage and her. She wanted to stay in that amazing place as long as possible, and clung to him as they descended from their sensual high.

"I can't get enough of you," she whispered. "You make me want more and more."

"Same for me," he said, cradling her against him.

"You feel so good," she said, wiggling even closer. "Hold me like this forever."

He didn't respond and Lissa understood. She was asking more than he could give. She was asking more than *she* could give.

The next morning she and Gage awakened. "Can you do me a favor after lunch?" she asked as she pulled him against her.

"What kind of favor?" he asked.

"You don't have to launch a spacecraft," she said.

"Well, that's good. Okay, I'll try. What time?" he asked.

"After lunch? Two-ish," she said.

"Okay. I can do that unless there's an emergency."

"Good," she said.

"What's up?"

"You'll find out at two-ish," she said with a grin.

He frowned in response. "I don't like surprises," he said.

"Hopefully you'll like this one," she said, mentally crossing her fingers.

"We'll see."

"Yeah, we will," she said.

Later that day, Gage received a call from Lissa.

"Hi," she said with breathless excitement in her voice. "It's almost two. Can you meet me at your place?"

"I guess," he said, curious about what she had going on. "Let me make sure Will can cover for me. I can't stay long," he warned.

"That's okay. I just need you for a few minutes," she said and giggled.

He heard a voice in the background. "Hey, where are you, anyway?"

"I'll see you soon," she said and hung up.

Gage shook his head as he rose from his desk. He walked toward Will. "I need to make a quick run back to my place. Can you cover for me? It shouldn't take long."

Will nodded. "No problem," he said. "Take as long as you need."

Vickie looked up from the dispatch desk. "You're going to your house?"

"Yeah," he said, trying to decipher her expression. She had her finger over her mouth as if she was trying to keep a secret.

"Well, have fun," she finally said and smiled.

Gage frowned. "I'll be back soon," he said and headed for his car. During the entire drive to his ranch, Gage racked his brain about what was going on. Lissa was acting too strange. Vickie was, too.

Pulling into his driveway, he started to stop at his trailer. Then he glanced past it to his house. A crowd of people stood in his yard with Lissa standing in front, a big smile stretching from ear to ear.

Gage got a sinking sensation in his gut. She shouldn't have done it, he thought. She shouldn't have gotten the volunteers to spend precious time fixing up his house when other people needed help more than he did.

He got out of his car and the whole group shouted, "Welcome home!"

Lissa rushed toward him. "I know you said you

didn't want it done, but you work so hard for everyone. You don't get very much time off," she said, talking fast. "We just thought that you should have a decent place to stay during the few hours that you're not working." She searched his face. "I hope you'll like it. I hope you're happy."

"I'm sure I'll like it," he said even though he couldn't quite tamp down his resentment. He thought he'd made it perfectly clear that he didn't want his house repaired yet. He wouldn't dare be ungrateful to the volunteers after all the work they'd done.

He took a deep breath and forced a smile. "Introduce me to these fine people and show me what you did."

She smiled and was so excited he would swear she was nearly bouncing. "As all of you know, this is Sheriff Gage Christensen. I hope all of you will introduce yourselves to him. Gage, I'd like you to meet this crew's leader, Tom Samuels."

"Nice to meet you," Gage said. "Thank you for all you've done for Rust Creek Falls and for me."

"We've had a good time," Tom said. "Come inside your house and take a look. As you know, your home was in better condition than most because you got rid of the wet stuff. We took care of the floor, hung some drywall and painted the downstairs. We replaced your linoleum with tile in the kitchen. Your new refrigerator and stove were delivered this morning. We decided we should let you select your own furniture," Tom added with a laugh. "Katie and some of the other ladies took care of your upstairs."

"Upstairs?" he said. "I didn't have any damage upstairs."

A middle-aged woman approached Gage. "Hello, I'm Katie. You didn't have any damage, but we just thought you'd enjoy it more if we dusted and cleaned up a little and washed your linens. It's a real honor to help turn your house back into a home, Sheriff. Everyone we talk to has nothing but praise for you."

A knot of guilt formed in his chest. At the same time, he was overwhelmed by what the volunteers had done for him and everyone else affected by the flood. "I don't know what to say except thank you," he said. "Thank you for this. Thank you for everything you've done for our community. It's people like you that make the world a better place. I think we should all give you a hand," he said and started to clap.

Lissa immediately joined in and the volunteers started clapping, too. It was a unique, joyous moment.

After that, the crowd got into a van and headed back to the church. They needed to pack up so they could begin their journey home. Lissa hung around, waving at the crew as they departed. She turned to him and he could see a bit of anxiety in her eyes.

"You're happy about this, aren't you?" she asked. "I know you said you wanted to be last in line for help, but—"

"You're right," he said. "I did want to be last in line. I don't deserve to get my house fixed when there are families still in need of repairs."

Her face fell. "But this really didn't take very long. The crew worked quickly, and other crews were working on other houses."

"Whatever time they spent on my house should have been spent on someone else's house," he said and sighed. "Thank you, but you shouldn't have." He turned and walked toward his SUV.

Feeling her staring after him, he turned around. "Come on. I'll give you a ride to town."

He helped her into the car and got into his side and started driving. Gage was in no mood for small talk and he sure as hell hoped Lissa would respect his silence. She did until they were about five minutes from town.

"I keep trying to figure out why you're upset about this," she said. "Because you *are* upset."

"I'm not upset," he said, but even Gage could hear the edge in his tone.

"Someone once said to me, it's better to give than to receive, and it's easier, too. I thought it was funny at the time, but I think it may be especially true for you."

He could feel her looking at him, but he focused on driving. Gage was feeling too much right now. Too much he just couldn't explain.

"I won't apologize for helping this happen. It seemed right to me. But I can say I'm sorry you're not happy about it. I really wanted to help make your life better," she said.

Gage hated the crack he heard in her usually peppy voice. "Lissa," he said.

She shook her head. "No. Please don't say any more," she said. "Just let me out at the rooming house."

They were close to town, but not close enough. Those two minutes of silence seemed like they lasted forever. He barely stopped the car before she hopped out. "Lissa," he tried again, not sure what he was going to say.

"'Bye. Hope the rest of your day goes well," she said and walked away.

Gage stared after her, feeling completely empty. How had that happened? How had she burst into his life and made him feel full and alive? And now she'd left him feeling like a jerk.

Well, maybe he was a jerk. What Lissa didn't understand, what nobody seemed to understand, was that Gage was still making up for what happened to Hunter McGee while Gage was out of town. Gage had a feeling he would spend the rest of his life making up for that moment when the mayor died.

Gage could tell that Lissa was avoiding him after the second day that she didn't come into the office. He couldn't blame her. He felt like he'd squashed a butterfly. She had just wanted to do something nice for him, but he just couldn't accept it. It was probably for the best, he told himself. She wouldn't be here forever and he'd already grown far too attached to her. She made his world feel lighter and brighter and he could use that today, he thought, as he checked his watch. This wasn't the first time, nor would it be the last, that he'd drive Thelma McGee to visit her son's grave.

Gage picked up Thelma from the mayor's office. Although every white hair was in place and she was neatly dressed, Thelma seemed a bit more frail today. Trying to keep up her son's tradition of caring for the citizens of Rust Creek Falls was clearly taking a toll on her. Today she carried plastic blue gerbera daisies.

"After that last snow, I feel like I have to go to plastic. Real flowers turn into brown sticks so quickly, even more so when it's cold," she said, as if she felt the need to explain herself as Gage drove toward the cemetery.

"I'm sure Hunter's looking down, glad to see some bright colors on his grave," he said.

Thelma smiled. "Hunter always liked bright colors. When he was a boy, he wanted to paint his room red. At first, I refused. I was afraid he would never go to sleep in such a bright room. Then I gave in and allowed him to paint one wall red. He had such energy. It was hard to refuse him."

Gage nodded. "That's part of the reason he was such a good mayor. That and the fact that he had a vision for Rust Creek Falls."

He turned into the small cemetery and drove to Hunter's grave then helped Thelma out of the car.

"You're very kind to bring me here, Gage," she said.

"I'm glad to be here for you," he said, offering his arm as they took the few steps to the grave. His gut twisting in remorse and guilt, he removed his hat out of respect.

Thelma bowed her head in what Gage suspected was a silent prayer. She bent to place the flowers on the grave.

"Let me do that," he said and took the flowers. He placed them in front of the small headstone.

Thelma pressed her lips together and nodded. "We can leave now."

Gage escorted her back to the car. "I'm so sorry, Thelma. If there was any way I could go back in time and make sure I was here so that Hunter wouldn't have—" He broke off and shook his head.

"Gage, you couldn't have prevented my son's death," she said, looking into his eyes. "You're not thinking this through. Hunter was always in the thick of things. He was a man of the people. Do you really think he would have just stayed at home during a flash flood while people were in danger? You could have had yourself and the whole cavalry, but that wouldn't have been enough for him. He wouldn't be able to sit still if there was a chance he could help or save someone." Thelma put her hand on his arm. "I hate it and I don't understand it, but it was just his time. You're not doing anyone any favors trying to take responsibility for his death. You just need to face the fact that God is more important than you are, and He wanted Hunter with Him in heaven."

Gage was surprised at Thelma's response. She was usually so sweet and mild. He felt as if he was getting a lecture from a teacher. It was the equivalent of a hard mental shake.

"Now, would you please take me to get some wings?" she asked. "I'm hungry and Hunter would definitely approve. He loved wings."

Gage smiled. "It would be my pleasure," he said and drove back to town.

After the meal, Gage drove Thelma home and he returned to the office. He was in no mood to go to his own home tonight. Too many thoughts swimming in his brain.

Walking in the door, he waved to Vickie. She was getting ready to leave for the day. The phone rang and she made a face. "Okay, but this is the last one I'm taking," she muttered and picked up the phone. "Sheriff's office." She paused a long moment. "Oh, no. Not Lissa."

Lightning might as well have struck Gage. He immediately turned to look at Vickie. The dispatcher was furiously taking notes. "They've taken her to the clinic in the next county. They may have to move her to Livingston if she doesn't improve," she repeated. "Unconscious," she whispered, wincing and shaking her head. "What happened?"

She lifted her index finger to Gage. "Unsecured beams. They fell on her. Oh, no," she said. "I'll relay the message."

Gage was already headed out the door. He was pretty sure his heart had stopped when he'd heard Lissa's name. How had this happened? Maybe it wouldn't have if he hadn't been trying to ignore her. He thought the next crew wasn't coming in until tomorrow.

His mind racing, he drove to the clinic. He called ahead for an update but the receptionist wouldn't give him any information because he wasn't a relative. Swearing under his breath, he walked in the door to the clinic. He wasn't going to put up with any bull about not being able to see her. She had come to his town and he was responsible for her as long as she was here.

He approached the receptionist, a sour-looking woman with pointy glasses. "I'm Sheriff Christensen and I'm here to see Lissa Roarke," he said in a firm voice.

She looked him over and not in a nice way. "I'll have to check with the doctor," she said. "I've received several inquiries about her." She walked away and it was all Gage could do not to follow the woman down the hall.

She returned and met his gaze. "The doctor said you can see her in a few minutes. They're still sewing her stitches."

His stomach turned. "Stitches?" he echoed.

"Yes. She'll have quite a few and be black and blue over much of her face and head. But that's all I'm going to say. You'll have to talk to Miss Roarke about her condition. We have policies, you know," she said.

"Then she's conscious?" he asked.

The receptionist frowned. "Yes, she is. That is all I'm going to say. You can take a seat."

Take a seat? Gage had barely been able to sit in his vehicle during the drive over here. He wasn't going to be able to sit until he saw with his own eyes that Lissa was okay.

Eleven minutes and thirty-seven seconds later,

the receptionist waved to him. "You can come back now," she said and led him to an examination room near the end of the hall.

A man and woman dressed in scrubs stood on either side of Lissa, who was flat on her back on a gurney. "We'll have to transfer you to the hospital in Livingston if you don't have someone who can stay with you for the next twenty-four hours," the doctor was saying.

"She can stay with me," Gage said. "I'll look after her."

All three turned to look at him. "Sheriff Gage Christensen," he said, extending his hand to the man who'd been talking when he entered the room.

"Dr. Keller," the man said, returning the handshake. "This is Nurse Benson. Miss Roarke took quite a blow to the head. She was unconscious and will need to be monitored."

Lissa tried to raise up on her elbows. "I'm really much better," she said.

The nurse gently pushed her back down. "You need to keep your head lower to reduce the chance of swelling."

Lissa sighed. "I've got a crew of volunteers arriving tomorrow and I have to brief them and plan—"

"We'll find someone else to cover for you tomorrow and the day after that, if necessary," Gage said to her. It was hard seeing her like this, her face pale except for the bruises already forming, stitches sewn across the gash on her forehead. "If you're sure she can go home, I'll take care of her. Just give me the instructions."

A few minutes later, Gage carefully loaded Lissa into his SUV and put her seat into the recline position.

"I'm really better," she said.

"I'm glad," he said. "But the doctor said you have to rest for a minimum of twenty-four hours. And I know you're going to cooperate, because otherwise you'll have to go to the hospital."

Lissa frowned but didn't argue. "I just don't know what to do about that incoming crew of volunteers," she fretted. "I need to get them pumped up so they can hit the ground running tomorrow."

"Well, you aren't going to be hitting the ground or running for a few days. The doctor said you have to get complete rest, then you can gradually become more active. Gradually," he repeated.

"I don't have time to be gradual," she said in a cranky voice.

"You don't have a choice," he said. "I wish you hadn't gone out to that house by yourself. If I'd been with you, that beam wouldn't have fallen on you."

He felt her gaze on him. "What? Oh, for crying out loud, Gage. Do you think you're responsible for everything? Well, of course you are. Did you hear about that meteorite that went past the earth? You were behind that, weren't you? And that tsunami in the Pacific. What were you thinking? Why didn't you stop that? Along with global warming. Sheesh," she said. "Accidents happen. You see them all the time and you know it's just part of life."

Gage felt a hard twist of discomfort. Lissa sounded an awful lot like Thelma McGee.

"It's my job to take care of my people. How am I supposed to stop being protective?"

"I'm not saying you shouldn't be protective. That's one of the reasons I—" She broke off. "One of the reasons I admire you. But you can't control everything. You can't prevent every accident or natural disaster."

Gage sat with that for a moment. Maybe she and Thelma were right. Maybe he needed to ease off a little bit. "Well, I have to admit, I think I'd have a hard time fighting off a tsunami."

She giggled. "You think?"

It was so good to hear her little laugh. Gage still hadn't let down his guard since he'd seen her. If Lissa wasn't alive somewhere in this world, he didn't know what he would do.

Gage took her to the house. "I'm carrying you," he insisted. "You don't need to take those steps."

"This is ridiculous," she said. "You're going to get a hernia."

He chuckled. "If I do, it will be for a good cause," he said, as he carried her up the flight of stairs to the second floor

"You need to put me down," she said.

"Not until I get you to the bed."

"I need to use the restroom," she said.

"Oh," he said, and set her down at the door to the bathroom. "I'll be here if you need anything."

"I think I can handle this," she said, closing the door in his face.

In a snippy mood, he thought, waiting patiently. A couple moments later, she opened the door. "I would like to walk to the bedroom myself," she told him.

He sighed. "Okay." He followed behind her and when she sat down on the bed, he kneeled down to pull off her boots. He looked up at her to find her looking at him with a soft expression on her face. "I've missed you," she said.

He rose and sat beside her. "I've missed you, too." Reining in the feelings that ripped through him, he leaned forward and brushed a gentle kiss on her cheek. "Let's not waste any more time fighting."

She took a deep breath and let it out. "That sounds good to me."

"I'm glad we agree. Now lie down and don't get up unless I tell you that you can," he said sternly.

Glowering at him, she reclined on the bed. "You don't have to be nasty about it."

"I'm not being nasty, I'm being firm. I'm in charge of you for the next twenty-four hours. That means you have to do what I tell you to do," he said.

"There was a time when you would find another way to keep me busy in your bed," she said with a smile too sexy for a woman with stitches on her head.

"Don't tempt me," he told her and hoped the next twenty-four hours of not making love to her didn't kill him.

Chapter Ten

Gage received no less than twelve offers from people who wanted to help. Three from men who offered to take over sitting with her so he could work. Jared Winfree, who'd caused so much trouble at the bar, even had the nerve to call the office and say he wanted to know where he could take some flowers.

"You can tell him the only flowers he's gonna see are from pushing up daisies if he tries to come anywhere near Lissa," Gage told Vickie heatedly.

"Okay, calm down," she said. "But we're getting a ton of food and we need to do something with it. You want me to bring some by the house?" Vickie asked.

Gage nodded. "Sure. That will be fine. I've been feeding her canned soup, but I think she may be ready for something else soon."

"Okay, now let me talk to Lissa," she said.

"She can't talk," he said. "She's resting." More than likely she was bored out of her mind because he wouldn't let her have either her cell phone or iPad.

"I'll stop by the rooming house and pick up a few things for her. She might like a change of clothes."

"Thanks," he said. "We'll be here."

Lissa would hit the twenty-four hour post-concussion mark in just a few hours, but Gage was going to try to keep her down as long as he could. She'd rested well last night and he'd woken her every three hours just as the doctor had instructed. He'd noticed her touching her forehead as if it hurt, but whenever he asked, she denied it. Instead of arguing, he just gave her a cool cloth.

An hour later, Lissa awakened and a few minutes after that, Vickie knocked at the door. "Come on in," he said to Vickie. "It's nice of you to bring us some food."

"I couldn't subject Lissa to your idea of food after she'd been injured," Vickie said and headed for the kitchen armed with bags and a tote with clothing. Gage relieved her of the bags.

"Let me talk to her," Lissa called from the bedroom. "I'll come downstairs."

"No, you won't," he said, but Lissa was already making her way down the stairs.

"I want to see Vickie," she said.

"Hey there, girl," Vickie said and grimaced. "Oh, my goodness. That beam got you good, didn't it?"

"Is it that bad? I haven't looked today," Lissa said.

"Nothing a ball cap and some makeup won't cover. I brought you a change of clothes and some food. Now sit down before Gage throws a conniption," she said, urging Lissa into a kitchen chair.

"Do you know anything about the new crew? Gage took away my phone," she said in disgust.

"You wouldn't rest if I didn't remove all communication devices and we both know it," he said. "What do you want to drink? I have soda and water."

"Soda," she said, pressing her right eyebrow.

"Oh, look, her head is hurting," Vickie said. "Can she take anything?"

"Not much at the moment," he said. "They told me to give her cool washcloths," he said and dampened a fresh one for her.

"Thank you. It does help," she said then turned to Vickie. "He really has been very gentle."

"Well, I hope so. I'd hate to hear he was being a

cranky pants," Vickie said. "Your new volunteers arrived and the pastor is going to fill in for you the next few days."

"That's nice of him," Lissa said. "Do you know where they're planning to go first tomorrow? Are the lunches prepared for them? And—"

Vickie held up her hand. "I'm sure everything is taken care of. You've got this whole thing running like a well-oiled machine. The local people are coming out of the woodwork asking what they can do."

Lissa smiled. "I know there are good people all over the world, but you guys from Rust Creek Falls keep surprising me."

"Well, we've taken a pretty big shine to you, too. Some of us wouldn't mind if you stayed. Right, Gage?" Vickie hinted.

Gage plastered a confused expression on his face. "Huh?"

"Yeah, huh," Vickie said. "Listen, I've got to go. Will told me to tell you that everything's been pretty quiet if you need to take off another day."

"No. I'll be in tomorrow. I'm taking Lissa to the rooming house and Melba has agreed to look out for her."

"I don't need to have anyone look after me. I'm better," she said.

Vickie leaned toward her and patted her hand.

"Sweetie, you haven't looked in the mirror. You need a little more rest."

Lissa shrugged. "I may look bad, but I feel fine."

"Well, you wouldn't want to scare any of those volunteers," Vickie said and stood.

"Gee, thanks," Lissa said.

"You wouldn't want me to lie," Vickie said with a mischievous grin. "Y'all enjoy the food. That apple cobbler looks to die for. I almost kept it for myself. Bye now."

As soon as Vickie left, Gage dug into the bags of food. "Hey, there's turkey and dressing in here. Beef stew and some rolls and—"

A scream rent the air. Gage whipped around saw that Lissa was no longer sitting in the kitchen. He raced toward the bathroom. Lord, he hoped she hadn't fallen again.

He found her staring in horror into the mirror. "What's wrong?" he asked.

"I look like Frankenstein," she wailed.

He chuckled. "Not really," he said and stepped behind her. "You don't have those weird little bolts sticking out of your neck."

She shot him a sideways glance. "No wonder you've been acting like you're afraid I'll break. Let me see what else Vickie brought. I hope she tucked some concealer in that bag somewhere."

"You don't need to be worrying about how you look. Especially tonight. You need to keep resting."

"My twenty-four hours is up," she said.

"You still need to take things slow. I know it's hard for you, but you've got to be lazy."

"And how would you respond if someone told you to be lazy?"

"The same way you are," he said and gently pulled her against him. "That's why I understand how hard this is for you."

"Thanks for taking care of me. I guess I'm not the best patient."

"Don't worry. You'll be as good as new soon enough," he promised. "Just try not to rush it. Everyone wants you back at full throttle."

After a filling dinner and dessert, Gage returned Lissa's electronic devices to her. She made a few calls and sent several text messages then she took a break. "Everyone's telling me to rest," she said.

"Let's do something we haven't done together before," he said.

She smiled at him. "What would that be?"

"Watch some television," he said.

Lissa punched at him.

Lissa might fight the rest, but Gage noticed she fell asleep on his shoulder halfway through the show they were watching. Gage carried her upstairs and laid her down on the bed.

Her eyelids fluttered open. "Hi," she said.

His heart turned over. She had no idea how pretty she was even with bruises and stitches.

"You don't want to kiss me because I look like Frankenstein," she said.

He lowered his head and took her mouth in a deep caress. "I always want to kiss you, Lissa."

The next day, Gage checked in on Lissa every other hour. By the fourth time he called, she sounded irritated. Chuckling, he hung up the phone and went on patrol to give Will a well-deserved break. On the way back, he filled up his gas tank and spotted Collin Traub doing the same thing. Collin had not only lassoed Gage's sister's heart—he and Willa had been married at the end of July—he had also thrown his hat in the ring as a candidate for mayor of Rust Creek Falls.

Although Gage had voiced his support for Collin, he knew he was supposed to appear more neutral than not. That didn't mean he couldn't warn his future brother-in-law about what he'd heard about the Crawford family. "Hey, man, come here," he called to Collin.

Collin waved then finished filling up his tank and pulled to the side. He strode toward Gage. "How's it going? I know you've been working double time lately. And did I hear the volunteer coordinator from New York got hurt recently?"

"Yeah. She's a pistol, but she was no match for that beam that fell on her," Gage said.

"Ouch," Collin said with a wince. "Will she be okay?"

"If she'll slow down a little bit," Gage grumbled. "But there's another reason I waved you over. As you know, I'm supposed to be neutral on this election, but I thought it was fair for you to know that I'm hearing rumors that the Crawfords are working on a smear campaign on you. Handle that information however you see fit."

Collin nodded with a serious expression and shook Gage's hand. "Thanks. You're a good man."

"I try," Gage said dryly. "Take care, now," he said. "And take care of my sister."

Collin's expression softened. "You know how I feel about your sister," he said.

"Yeah, I know," Gage said, pushing down a twist of irritation. Romance was easy for other folks, but not for him.

Lissa tried to rest, but it was torture when she wanted to be with her volunteer crew. And everyone was so chintzy with the information they provided. "Go rest," they all said. "We're all fine." It was all she could do not to spy.

She'd promised Gage, however, that she would rest, and she was doing her best. He'd taken her back to the rooming house so Melba could check on her every couple of hours, which prevented Lissa from getting into too much trouble.

When she looked at the calendar, she felt sick to her stomach. Her assignment with Bootstraps would be over soon. There was still so much to do. If she were truthful, she couldn't bear the thought of leaving the people of Rust Creek Falls. Even more, she hated the thought of not being close to Gage. He was the most amazing man she'd ever met and she didn't want to lose him.

With that in mind, she wrote a heartfelt email to her supervisor at Bootstraps, pleading for an extension of her time in Rust Creek Falls. She could only hope her supervisor would agree with her.

Just when Lissa was sure she was going stir-crazy from staying inside all day, Melba knocked at her door. "There's a young man who wishes to see you," she said.

"Who would that be?"

"Why, Gage, of course," Melba said.

Lissa slowly went down the stairs to find him at the front door. "Hi," she said. "Nice to see you. What's the occasion?"

"I'm taking you back to my house with me," he said. "Melba took care of you today, but I'll take care of you tonight."

Her heart turned over at the expression in his eyes. How could she leave such an amazing man?

The next morning, Gage took her to the rooming house, but Lissa slapped on some concealer and a ballcap and headed over to the church to meet the volunteers. She knew she probably shouldn't spend the whole day out with them, but she couldn't resist the urge to be with the people who were doing so much for Rust Creek Falls.

She greeted the pastor and his face fell. "Oh, my goodness, Miss Roarke, you must go back to your room and rest," he said. "You're clearly not well yet."

Well, darn, Lissa thought. *So much for rallying the troops.* She needed better concealer.

She went back to her room and moped. How interesting that Gage had never looked at her with horror over her bruises and Frankenstein stitches. Without saying a word, he made her feel beautiful every time he looked at her.

The following day, Lissa went to the general store wearing sunglasses and bought every concealer they carried. Perhaps she should order over the internet. She checked out and the cashier studied her.

"Are you Lissa Roarke, the charity woman from New York?" the cashier asked.

"Yes," Lissa said hesitantly. "I recently had a little accident and I'm trying to conceal the bruises."

"Let me see," the woman said.

Lissa reluctantly lifted her sunglasses and the woman widened her eyes.

"Ouch," she said. "Looks like it was more than a little accident. Yellow for a blue bruise, but the colors will change. After that, green for red bruises. And bangs are your friend."

"How do you know this?" Lissa asked.

The cashier's gaze darkened. "Bad experience. Never to experience again."

"Good for you," Lissa said. "If anything other than a beam hits you in the future, please call me."

The cashier tilted her head. "I'll do that. Good luck with the bruises."

"Thanks," Lissa said and left the general store. That was one more person with whom she felt a bond in Rust Creek Falls. The numbers were racking up.

Lissa did more work on her iPad, but also took a few mininaps. She was surprised how tired she was. Again, at the end of the day, Gage picked her up and took her back to his house.

She felt more energetic than she had felt in days as she walked into his house. "Think you can make love to Frankenstein?" she challenged.

"I've been counting the minutes," he said and carried her up to his bed. He made love to her sweetly and tenderly and she fell asleep in his arms.

Lissa watched her email daily, anxious to get a response from her supervisor giving her more time in Rust Creek Falls. In the meantime, she followed the clerk's instructions and painted the upper half of her face with yellow. Wearing sunglasses, she met the volunteers the next morning.

She saw several people trying to look past her sunglasses, but tried to distract them. When one person was clearly not listening to her, she finally said, "I have bruises. They're ugly. I'm trying to protect you."

"I can deal with it," the man said.

Lissa lifted her sunglasses.

The man winced. "Okay."

"Yeah, give me a break," she said. "How are the repairs going?"

"Good. We would love to be able to place furniture," he said.

"It's coming in the next few days," she said.

The man nodded. "Are you single?"

"Not really," she said, but she appreciated the compliment of being asked.

Lissa visited the different crews by midday and tried to motivate them. She hated how tired she got by midafternoon, but surrendered to her weariness and took a nap. By evening, she was refreshed.

Gage took her to his ranch again. This was becoming a habit. A habit she wanted to continue. They made love again and again throughout the night, though he was utterly gentle with her.

When Lissa awakened the next morning, she was eager to check her email. Surely her supervisor would have made a decision. Hopefully Lissa would be staying another month. She couldn't imagine anything different.

Lissa met with her volunteers and worked with them for a while. By midafternoon, she was pooped and stretched out on her bed at Melba's.

Lissa checked her email again and this time she saw a message from her boss in her inbox. Mentally crossing her fingers, she held her breath and read the email.

Dear Lissa,

We're very impressed with all you have accomplished in Montana. You have far exceeded our expectations and we believe the people of Rust Creek Falls have benefitted greatly from your service there. Because of the progress you've made and also because Bootstraps plans to make a cash donation to the fund for the new school in Rust Creek Falls, we believe it's time to turn our attention and resources to other areas.

That means we will want you to return to New York within the next week as originally planned. Again, thank you for your service in Montana. We look forward to placing you in a position as lead coordinator for another project very soon.

Lissa couldn't believe her eyes. Her supervisor had turned her down flat. She wouldn't even have an extra week. How could she wrap everything up so quickly? How could she leave these people she'd come to love? How could she leave Gage?

Her hands shook with emotion and a knot of misery formed in her throat. What was she going to do?

She was so upset she couldn't imagine talking to anyone, especially Gage. Suddenly the room felt too small so she put on a jacket and took a walk. Her mind swirling with confusion, she tried to think of a solution. Perhaps she could go back to New York and visit Gage occasionally. Even as she considered the possibility, she knew it wouldn't work. She couldn't help wondering if Gage would lose interest if she left. He was so busy. It was a challenge for him to maintain a relationship with her when she was in town let alone when she was on the other side of the country.

She wondered if she should quit her job and start over here in Rust Creek Falls. The trouble was the lack of positions. Plus, she wasn't totally sure Gage would want her to stay. He'd said from the beginning that their relationship was temporary. He'd seemed to accept that fact a lot more easily that she had.

Her cell phone rang, distracting her from her thoughts. She glanced at the caller ID. Gage. She couldn't talk to him. Not yet. She had to figure this out.

Lissa successfully dodged him by going to the church and helping to serve the evening meal for the volunteers. Both they and the pastor were excited with their progress. It was all she could do to hold herself together and praise them for their work and contributions. The pastor hovered over her, encouraging her to go rest. She dragged out the cleanup, but couldn't delay returning to the rooming house after that.

Entering from the back door, she climbed the steps to her room. Thank goodness she'd successfully avoided both Melba and Gage. She opened her door to find Gage sitting in the chair in her room.

She gaped at him in surprise.

"Where the hell have you been, darlin'?" Gage asked. "I've been worried about you."

All her emotions converged on her at once and she burst into tears. "I have terrible news," she said. "Terrible, terrible news."

Immediately on his feet, Gage pulled her into his arms. "Whoa. What's wrong? Did you hear something bad from the doctor? Did you faint or get sick?"

Lissa shook her head. "No, no. Nothing like that." She swallowed hard over her tight throat. "I heard from my boss. I asked her if I could extend my stay here in Rust Creek Falls. She said no," she said, her voice betraying how upset she felt. "I have to leave in a week."

Gage gave a slow nod. He looked away and sighed. "We knew this was coming."

"Yes, but I wanted to stop it," she said. "Or at least delay it."

"I don't like it, either, but we both knew it from the start. Maybe it's for the best," he said. "Not to drag it out and quit while things are good."

She stared at him in surprise. "For the best. How could it possibly be for the best? I've fallen in love with you. I thought you had strong feelings for me. Was I wrong?"

"No," he said, squeezing her arm then backing away. He raked his hand through his hair. "Lissa, I love the way you look at me right now, but what's going to happen if you stick around for a while? I'm not the cowboy hero you think I am. Life is not like an old Western. I'm not perfect. I'm just a man and I'm bound to screw up sometimes. What's going to happen then?"

Confused, she shook her head. "We'll work it out."

"I'll tell you what's going to happen. We won't be working it out. You'll be walking out," he said with grim confidence. "Maybe it's better for us to split while we still have good memories."

Lissa head was spinning from his words. "Is

that all I am to you? A fond memory for your scrapbook?"

Gage rested his hands on his hips and glanced away then back at her. "Listen, you need to know that I saw what you wrote about me. I wasn't snooping. I'd brought your iPad back in the house and you were on the phone. The document came right up." He shook his head. "That man you wrote about. He isn't me. You don't really know me at all."

Anger rushed through her. "Maybe I just know you better than you think you know yourself."

"Lissa—"

The threat of tears too great, she lifted her hands and shook her head. "Stop. I think you've said enough."

Gage sighed and looked at her for a long moment. "I guess I'd better go."

"I guess you'd better," she said.

Chapter Eleven

It was all Lissa could do not to leave town right away. Her heart felt as if it had been ripped from her chest. She felt so deceived. But maybe she had deceived herself. Maybe Gage hadn't felt nearly as strongly about her as she had about him. The realization wounded her in such a way that she knew she'd never completely heal from it.

Wounded or not, she had a job to finish. The volunteers would be here for a few more days and Lissa was determined to maximize the time she had left to help as many residents as possible. Deciding she had fully recovered from her minor concussion, Lissa threw herself into repair work and avoided the sheriff's office. The good thing about hard work was that she was too tired by evening to think about how miserable she was.

The night before the volunteers were to leave town, a thank-you banquet was held for them. Lissa gave her last speech of gratitude and had to tamp down her emotions. It began to hit her hard that she would be leaving in just two days. Blinking back the tears, she gave a special thank-you to the pastor of the church and his congregation for all their assistance.

As she sat down, she noticed some familiar faces standing in the back of the room. Will, the deputy sheriff, nodded toward her. Vickie, the dispatcher waved. Gage helped Thelma McGee into a chair. The sight of Gage made her heart twist so hard she had to look away. What were they doing here? From her peripheral vision, she saw several other citizens she'd met during the past month. What was going on—

The pastor stood in front of the group. "We want to thank the volunteers for traveling from their homes and sleeping on cots, *when* you got to sleep," he added and several people laughed. Everyone knew they spent more time working than sleeping, and everyone was okay with it. "Our community is grateful for your service, and we pray that God will bless you from this experience."

He paused. "There is another person we want to thank and honor tonight, and that is Lissa Roarke."

Lissa stared in shock. She'd had no idea that

she was going to be the focus of the community's gratitude.

"She blew into town like a fast-moving train and inspired everyone around her. With her help, we accomplished much more for people here in Rust Creek who've been hurting and doing without for months. It has been my privilege to work by your side. And now, Mrs. Thelma McGee will make a special presentation," the pastor said.

Gage assisted Thelma to her feet and escorted her to the front of the room. Lissa forced herself not to look at Gage. If she even looked at him, she feared she would burst into tears. Instead she focused on Thelma and noticed that the woman was carrying a box.

"Hello, everyone," Thelma said.

"Hello," several in the crowd said in return.

Thelma smiled. "As most of you know, my son Hunter McGee was mayor for Rust Creek Falls for many years. He was a man devoted to the people and to our future, and we all miss him terribly. After the flood, I think some of us went into shock and we lost something. Something that Hunter always tried to instill in us, and that was hope. Lissa Roarke has not only facilitated repairs for dozens of people, she gave us something more important. Hope. Now I wish I could find a way to make her stay here in Rust Creek Falls, but I know she has to go back to New York."

Thelma opened the box and produced a large

key. "Before you leave, I've been given the honor by the town council to give Lissa Roarke the key to our town, Rust Creek Falls. You've won our hearts, Lissa. We'll never forget you."

Lissa's eyes filled with tears. Walking to the front where Thelma stood, Lissa swallowed hard to gain control, but she didn't know how she was going to do it. She embraced the woman and whispered, "Thank you."

"No," Thelma said and handed Lissa the key. "Thank *you*."

After that, people came to her in a blur, shaking her hand, offering words of gratitude and hugs. She noticed Gage standing behind the crowd, but she couldn't talk to him. She was still too hurt.

More than anything, she wanted to focus on the outpouring of love she was receiving. She wanted to save up the memory of all the wonderful people who thought she had done so much for them, but in truth, she had become so much richer by being with them for the past several weeks.

The crowd finally dwindled and Lissa grabbed her coat to leave. Gage walked toward her, but she put up her hand. "You take care of yourself," she said and quickly walked out the door.

She returned to the rooming house to pack. The day had been so busy she should have fallen asleep, but her mind was too full. Giving up on sleep,

Lissa turned on the light and opened her iPad and began to write.

She wrote about the wonderful people of Rust Creek Falls and how they sacrificed for each other. She wrote about Buddy buying the bunny for the little girl he didn't know. She wrote about the courage she'd seen and the determination to keep going even after the devastation they'd suffered. She wrote about Thelma and her devotion, along with that of Deputy Will. And yes, she also wrote about Gage. How could she not? She wrote for hours, and finally she felt as if she'd expressed at least some of her overwhelming thoughts and feelings about the people of Rust Creek Falls.

After that, it was as if at least part of her was a little more at peace, and she fell asleep for a couple hours. Her subconscious must have known she was leaving even though she was sleeping, because for once she was up before dawn. She made a copy of her revised article, put it into an envelope and ran to the sheriff's office and left it with the evening dispatcher.

Lissa returned to the rooming house and the last big breakfast that Melba would be making for her. She could hardly eat a thing.

"You haven't touched your food," Melba chided her.

"I don't eat as much when I travel," Lissa said. "Nerves, I guess. I appreciate you offering to take me to the airport."

"Well, of course I'll take you," Melba said. "Although all of us wish you were staying."

Lissa just pressed her lips together and remained silent. She didn't know what else could be said at this point, so she went upstairs to close her suitcase. Lissa loaded her luggage into Melba's big Buick and they headed for the airport in Livingston.

"Well, you've got a pretty day for travel," Melba said. "That's a good thing. Have you checked the weather in New York?"

Lissa shook her head, not really in the mood for small talk. But she should be polite. "I haven't," she said. "It's usually pleasant at this time of year, though."

"You'll have all those pretty fall colors from the leaves changing. We get the colors, but we also get the snow."

"That's true. I hadn't even thought about that," she said.

"Well, you've been so busy coordinating all those volunteers," Melba said. "We sure do appreciate you coming to Rust Creek Falls. I know we all hope you'll come back and visit."

Lissa's heart felt sore at the thought. "I don't know," she said. "I'll never forget Rust Creek Falls, but maybe it's best that I keep it as a memory." She thought about what she'd just said and smiled grimly. She sounded like Gage. That couldn't be good.

"You're thinking about a certain cowboy, aren't you?" Melba asked.

"Maybe," Lissa said softly, but remained quiet for the rest of the trip to the airport. Gage was a lost cause. There was nothing she could do. It was a ridiculous situation. She knew they were meant for each other, but Gage just wouldn't admit it.

Gage awoke early and couldn't get back to sleep, so he hauled himself out of bed, thinking he might as well get something done. Of course, maybe the reason he couldn't sleep was that he imagined he was smelling Lissa's sweet scent. He knew he couldn't be. The sheets on the bed had been changed and she hadn't been in his house for over a week. That was the way it was supposed to be, he told himself. That was the way it had to be.

He pulled on his clothes and took care of some early-morning chores. When he returned to the house, he saw a lone carton of yogurt in the fridge. The sight of it made him feel sad. Gage rolled his eyes. A yogurt carton was making him sad? He was losing his mind. Grabbing a frozen biscuit from the freezer, he tossed it in the microwave and told himself that it was time to get back to normal. Lissa Roarke was leaving this afternoon and she wasn't coming back. He'd helped make sure of it.

He drove into town, glancing at Strickland's Boardinghouse. He wondered if Lissa was up eating breakfast. He wondered what she would do before she left town. Gage was pretty sure she wouldn't stop by the office to say goodbye. The thought put him in even more of a dark mood.

Parking his car, he entered the office. Will wasn't there yet, but Vickie was at her desk. "Hey, the night dispatcher left this for you."

"What is it?" Gage asked, curious about the contents of the envelope with his name scrawled across the front of it.

"I don't know," Vickie said. "I'm nosy, but I don't open other people's correspondence."

Gage chuckled. "Okay. Anything I need to address first thing?"

"Nope. Everything's quiet so far," she said.

"Thanks," he said and went to grab a cup of coffee before he went into his office. Shrugging out of his coat, he pulled off his hat and sat down at his desk. He opened the envelope and read the top of the page. *An Essay on True Heroism by Lissa Roarke.* His gut tightened at the title, but he had to read it. He couldn't have torn his gaze from the page if he'd tried.

She wrote about the townspeople and how they sacrificed for each other. She wrote about the children and the teachers who had opened their homes in order to teach classes. She mentioned all sorts of details about the town that proved she had been watching very closely, and not with rose-colored glasses.

The more Gage read, the tighter his chest felt. His throat felt as if were tightening up, too. He rubbed his neck and chest. Lissa had poured her heart and soul into Rust Creek Falls. She'd handed him her heart and soul on a platter.

He continued reading and saw that the subject of the piece had turned to him. He felt a rush of discomfort.

The truth is that Sheriff Gage Christensen is one of the most important foundations of the Rust Creek Falls community. Everyone needs to be able to count on someone, and everyone counts on the sheriff. He shows up for everything from unexpected labor to helping with repairs and arresting a drug manufacturer trying to hide in the safe haven of his community. He's on call 24-7. He is a man dedicated to his people and his people are grateful for that dedication.

Some people might call the writer of this article biased when it comes to the subject of Gage Christensen, and they would be quite correct. I've had an opportunity to get to know him on a personal level, and he has taken care of me when I needed help. I'd like to end this essay with a thank-you to the cowboy who stole my heart. I don't want it back.

Overwhelmed by the depth of feeling in her words, Gage leaned back in the chair. Maybe Lissa had more insight than he'd believed. Maybe it wasn't such a bad thing that she thought he was a hero. Maybe she saw past his walls to the man he wanted to be.

How often does a man meet a woman like that? he wondered. How often would a woman like Lissa Roarke come into his life?

The answer hung over him like the blade of a guillotine. *Never,* he realized. He would *never* meet another woman like Lissa. Besides, he wouldn't want *another woman* like Lissa.

He would want Lissa.

The truth slapped him across the face. He'd lost her. Was there any way he could get her back? His mind started spinning. Maybe he could talk to her before she left. Maybe he could convince her.... Maybe.

Gage knew he was going to have to make a strong case for himself after the way he'd told her off. Rising from his desk, he called a friend in the next county who ran a business out of his home. His heart pounding in his chest, he was determined to get out there and back to Rust Creek Falls before Lissa left town.

Gage ran into Will as he headed out the door. "Hey, can you cover for me this morning?"

"Sure," Will said and looked at him with curiousity. "Problem?"

"I'm going to try to fix one before it's too late," Gage said.

Will gave a slow nod. "Is this about Lissa?"

"Yeah," Gage said.

"Good luck," Will said. "If I can't have her, then you're the next best thing."

Too focused to laugh, he headed out the door. He made it to his friend's house and bought the purchase of a lifetime for a man: a diamond ring. After all Gage had put Lissa though, he figured he was going to have to provide physical proof of his feelings for her.

As soon as he got back in his car, his cell rang. It was Will. "What's up?" Gage asked.

"I thought I should let you know that Lissa left early this morning. Melba Strickland took her to the airport. Lissa's flight is this morning."

Gage's stomach sank. "Do you know if she's gone?"

"I don't think so, but I'm not sure. You'd better head straight to Livingston," Will said.

"I'm on my way," Gage said, wondering if he had waited too late and his chance had passed.

At check-in, Lissa was told that her flight was running over an hour late, which only added to her bad mood. She didn't want to be leaving. Now the process was being dragged out even further. Lissa felt as if she were being tortured.

Melba, sweet as always, must have sensed how upset Lissa was and offered to wait with her since there was no need for Lissa to go through security yet. "We can have a cup of coffee or tea," Melba said.

"I don't want to inconvenience you," Lissa said.

"It's no problem," Melba said. "I'm happy to spend some time with you."

Lissa sipped a cup of tea while Melba drank coffee. With each passing moment, Lissa couldn't stop her thoughts of Gage.

She sipped her tea and tapped her foot, but the tea didn't calm her and her foot-tapping did nothing to relieve her of her nervous energy. "You know, Gage said that he and I were destined for failure," she finally said, unable to keep quiet any longer.

"Oh, really," Melba said. "I wonder why he said that."

"He said I was in love with a fantasy man. That I didn't love *him,* the real him," she said, still tapping her foot.

"That doesn't make much sense," Melba said. "You're a grown woman. You should know your mind. It's not as if you're a little girl."

"Exactly," Lissa said. "I'm a grown woman. He kept telling me something was going to go wrong one day and I was going to wake up and be totally disillusioned with him."

"Well, that could happen to any couple," Melba said. "You just have to make the decision you're going to stick together and work it out. I've had to do that with my husband and I've been married to him for over fifty years."

Lissa nodded, still irritated with how Gage had acted toward her the last time they'd talked. She didn't know when she would stop being irritated at him. "You know, now that I think about it, it was like Gage was asking for some kind of guarantee that nothing would ever go wrong between us. As much as I lo—" She broke off and cleared her throat. "As much as I had strong feelings for him, how could we never have an occasion when something would go wrong? It's not possible," she said, feeling herself get more worked up. "*That* is a fantasy. That's an even bigger fantasy. That you'll never have problems?" she scoffed.

Melba took another sip of her coffee. "Very true. Life is full of troubles. It's how you face them that counts."

"You know what?" she said. "I think Gage was scared."

"Really?" Melba said. "Well, you know you're a pretty girl. I wonder if he thought he couldn't keep you interested."

Unable to sit still another moment, Lissa stood. "That's it! That's it," she said. "He let me go because he was afraid of losing me. How ridiculous is that?"

Melba shook her head. "*Men*. Will they ever make sense?"

"Probably not," Lissa said. "But I'm not letting him get away with this. I'm going to confront him with the truth to his face."

Melba stared at her. "What are you going to do?"

"I'm cancelling my flight and I'm going to tell Gage Christensen that he can't fool me. I have him figured out from head to toe. I'm not backing down this time," she said and headed for the counter.

Midway through her conversation with the airline agent, she heard her name being called. By Gage.

"Lissa, Lissa, stop. You can't get on that plane," he yelled as he ran across the airport lobby.

Lissa saw him running toward her and felt as if she were having an out-of-body experience. She was so stunned she couldn't speak.

"You can't leave," he said as he got closer to her. "You'll regret it," he promised. "If not now, then soon. But you will regret it," he said.

The experience reminded her of something out of a movie. A crazy combination of nerves and excitement danced inside her. She didn't know whether to laugh or cry. A laugh bubbled from her throat and she was thankful she wasn't crying.

Gage glanced around and seemed to notice they were drawing a crowd. Based on his expression, he didn't care. He dropped to his knee in front of everyone.

Lissa gasped in surprise.

"I need to apologize for being such an ass," he said. "I know I hurt you and I'm sorry. I never, ever want to hurt you. You're too important to me," he said and took a deep breath. "I love you, Lissa Roarke. You're the best thing that's ever happened to me. I don't care if I have to follow you all the way to New York City. I'm never letting you go again."

Lissa could hardly believe her ears. She'd dreamed of Gage saying these things to her. She was almost afraid to believe it was true.

At that moment, he pulled a jeweler's box out of his pocket and opened it to display a diamond ring.

Her heart felt as if it had stopped in her chest. She shook her head.

His face fell. "You're saying no?"

"No," she said. "I mean…I'm just so surprised. How did this sudden turnaround happen?" she asked.

"It wasn't really sudden," he told her. "I think I've been in love with you since you first walked into my office. I just didn't trust that a sophisticated woman like you could really find happiness with a Rust Creek cowboy like me. But I read your essay this morning and I saw that you really do understand the town—and me." He shook his head. "Maybe *I'm* the one who was stereotyping you."

"Ya think?" she asked, still smarting from how much she'd suffered this past week. He had put her through hell. But the look of desperation on his face made her soften.

"Come on, sweet Lissa. Give this man a break."

She took a deep breath. "I think you'd better get up off that floor and kiss me," she said.

In a flash, he rose from his feet and pulled her into his arms and kissed her until her head was spinning.

She was so caught up in feeling Gage in her arms that she barely noticed the applause from the spectators.

Gage pulled back, his gaze latched on to hers. "Wait. Does that mean yes?"

"Yes, yes, yes," she said. "I'd already cancelled my flight. I just couldn't give you up without a fight."

"The only fighting I'm going to do is for us, not against us," he promised. He scooped her up in his arms and carried her out of the terminal. The crowd cheered behind them.

Epilogue

Gage pulled into the driveway and Lissa felt an overwhelming sense of relief. "I feel like I'm coming home," she said when he stopped his SUV.

Gage held her jaw gently with his hand and kissed her. "That's the way I always want you to feel. Always," he said.

She unlocked the door.

"Wait just a minute, there, city girl," he said and got out of the car and rounded to her side in a quick blur. He picked her up and carried her up the stairs to his house.

"What are you doing?" she asked. "You've done this before. You don't have to do it again."

"Honey, if it makes you happy, I'll be doing it until I can't walk. I just want to keep you happy," he said.

Lissa saw that he still wasn't sure of her. "You need to know that you can count on me. I'm not going to leave you even when things get rough. And they will because that's the way life is, full of ups and downs."

"It's just hard for me to believe that you could give up everything in New York for me," he said and guided her into the house.

"You still don't get it," she said. "You are the man I always wanted but never thought existed. I love you for who you are to everyone. Not just for how you act with me," she said. She stopped in the hallway. "I love you for who you are when no one is around because you're the best man I've ever met. And Gage, I know you're not perfect. You've acted like a jerk to me on more than one occasion."

He blinked. "Me? A jerk?"

She gave him a playful punch. "Yes, you," she said, laughing. "You've admitted it to me and apologized. That's one more reason for me to love you. It takes a wonderful man to admit when he's wrong."

"My only excuse is that falling for you made me crazy. I don't ever want to lose you or disappoint you," he said.

"You're stuck with me," she said. "In good and

bad times. But you may need to give me some winter driving lessons," she said.

"Oh, hell. You're gonna scare me to death if you go out on slippery roads," he said and led her upstairs.

"Then you need to teach me very thoroughly," she said.

"You can be sure I will," he said and started to undress her next to his bed. "I kept dreaming I could smell your perfume," he told her. "I thought I was going nuts. I missed you so much."

"I missed you, too," she said. "I don't want to ever be apart from you, Gage."

"I'll do my best to make that happen," he said and gently put her down on the bed. "I love you and I'm gonna make sure you never forget it."

He kissed her lips then caressed her body and made love to her for the whole afternoon. Lissa was so full of him and his love that she lost track of time. Finally, they came up for air.

A bit of reality slipped in. "I'm going to have to find a job," she said.

"I can support you," he said. "I don't want you to worry about that right now. You'll have enough of an adjustment to make getting through a Montana winter and becoming my wife."

His wife. The words made her dizzy. "I can't wait for it all. You and I are going to have a wonderful life, Gage."

"Honey, you've already made me the happiest man in the world. I can't imagine being any happier."

"Then I'll just have to try a little harder, won't I?" she said, snuggling against him.

"Well, you are a high achiever," he said with a wink. "I think I'd better kiss you again," he said.

"I think you'd better," she said, and knew she had found her true man, and her true home.

* * * * *

Don't miss MARRYING DR. MAVERICK
by Karen Rose Smith,
the next installment in the new
Special Edition continuity
MONTANA MAVERICKS:
RUST CREEK COWBOYS
On sale October 2013, wherever
Harlequin books are sold.

COMING NEXT MONTH FROM

H HARLEQUIN®

SPECIAL EDITION

Available September 17, 2013

HSECNM0913

REQUEST YOUR FREE BOOKS!

2 FREE NOVELS PLUS 2 FREE GIFTS!

♦ HARLEQUIN®

SPECIAL EDITION

Life, Love & Family

YES! Please send me 2 FREE Harlequin® Special Edition novels and my 2 FREE gifts (gifts are worth about $10). After receiving them, if I don't wish to receive any more books, I can return the shipping statement marked "cancel." If I don't cancel, I will receive 6 brand-new novels every month and be billed just $4.74 per book in the U.S. or $5.24 per book in Canada. That's a savings of at least 14% off the cover price! It's quite a bargain! Shipping and handling is just 50¢ per book in the U.S. and 75¢ per book in Canada.* I understand that accepting the 2 free books and gifts places me under no obligation to buy anything. I can always return a shipment and cancel at any time. Even if I never buy another book, the two free books and gifts are mine to keep forever.

235/335 HDN F45Y

Name _____ (PLEASE PRINT)

Address _____ Apt. #

City _____ State/Prov. _____ Zip/Postal Code

Signature (if under 18, a parent or guardian must sign)

Mail to the Harlequin® Reader Service:
IN U.S.A.: P.O. Box 1867, Buffalo, NY 14240-1867
IN CANADA: P.O. Box 609, Fort Erie, Ontario L2A 5X3

Want to try two free books from another line?
Call 1-800-873-8635 or visit www.ReaderService.com.

* Terms and prices subject to change without notice. Prices do not include applicable taxes. Sales tax applicable in N.Y. Canadian residents will be charged applicable taxes. Offer not valid in Quebec. This offer is limited to one order per household. Not valid for current subscribers to Harlequin Special Edition books. All orders subject to credit approval. Credit or debit balances in a customer's account(s) may be offset by any other outstanding balance owed by or to the customer. Please allow 4 to 6 weeks for delivery. Offer available while quantities last.

Your Privacy—The Harlequin® Reader Service is committed to protecting your privacy. Our Privacy Policy is available online at www.ReaderService.com or upon request from the Harlequin Reader Service.

We make a portion of our mailing list available to reputable third parties that offer products we believe may interest you. If you prefer that we not exchange your name with third parties, or if you wish to clarify or modify your communication preferences, please visit us at www.ReaderService.com/consumerschoice or write to us at Harlequin Reader Service Preference Service, P.O. Box 9062, Buffalo, NY 14269. Include your complete name and address.

HSE13R

*Jasmine "Jazzy" Cates looked at her time volunteering
in Rust Creek Falls as an escape from the familiarity
of Thunder Canyon. A fresh start. After a few months in
town with no luck, she was about to give up. And then
Brooks Smith, a sexy local veterinarian, makes a
surprising proposal that just might solve all their problems...*

***

Brooks knew he must be crazy.

Today he was going to marry a woman he was severely
attracted to, yet he didn't intend to sleep with her! If that
wasn't crazy, he didn't know what was.

He adjusted his tux, straightened his bolo tie, wishing all to
heck that Jazzy hadn't almost knocked his boots off last night
when he'd seen her in that red dress. And when he pushed
her chair in and saw that hole in the back of it...and her skin
peeking through, he'd practically swallowed his tongue.

There was a rap on the door. He was in the anteroom
that led to the nursery area in the back of the church. He
knew Jazzy was in a room across the vestibule that was used
exactly for situations like this—brides and their bridesmaids
preparing for a wedding.

Preparing for a wedding.

After the dinner last night, and the suspicious and wary
glances of her family, he'd retreated inward. He knew that. He
also knew it had bothered Jazzy. But how could he explain to
her that she turned him on more than he'd ever wanted to be

turned on? How could he explain to her that this marriage of convenience might not be so convenient, not when it came to them living together?

Still, he was determined to go through with this. Their course was set. He wasn't going to turn back now.

***

We hope you enjoyed this sneak peek from author Karen Rose Smith's new Harlequin® Special Edition book, MARRYING DR. MAVERICK, the next installment in MONTANA MAVERICKS: RUST CREEK COWBOYS, the brand-new six-book continuity launched in July 2013!

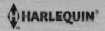

SPECIAL EDITION

Life, Love and Family

Look for the next and final book in the
Welcome to Destiny miniseries!

Recovering from a horrific crash has Devlin Murphy
fighting old demons physically, mentally and
emotionally. Is Tanya Reeves, with her alternative
healing ways, the answer to his prayers...or a
danger to his heart?

FLIRTING WITH DESTINY
by *USA TODAY* bestselling author
Christyne Butler

*Available October 2013 from
Harlequin® Special Edition® wherever books are sold.*